Furthe

"You can see, sme … Journal

"Has the atmosphere and the feeling that attracts all sorts of readers." *—Cleveland Plain Dealer*

"The best modern novel about the West."
—Jack Schaefer, author of Shane

"Has honesty, truth (which is something different) and gusto."
—Saturday Review

"It is a splendid portrayal, done with poignancy and restraint."
—Nashville Banner

"As fine a first book as a reviewer is apt to encounter."
—Baltimore Sun

"It has an atmosphere which is authentic and which brings a new and strange talent to American writing."
—New Haven Register

"Done with a master hand . . . with something of that accurate portrayal of folkways and vernacular which is one of the chief charms of Faulkner and Steinbeck." *—Buffalo Evening News*

"For all its freshness of youth, has a maturity and a literary quality that inherits from the great classical traditions."
—Santa Barbara News-Press

"An addition to American letters."
—Stephen Vincent Benét

BY ROBERT EASTON

NOVELS

The Happy Man
The Hearing
The Saga of California® Series
This Promised Land
Power and Glory
Blood and Money (forthcoming)

BIOGRAPHY

Max Brand: The Big Westerner
Lord of Beasts: The Saga of Buffalo Jones (with Mackenzie Brown)

HISTORY

Black Tide: The Santa Barbara Oil Spill and Its Consequences
The Book of the American West (with Jay Monaghan and others)

NATURAL HISTORY

California Condor: Vanishing American (with Dick Smith)

TRAVEL AND ADVENTURE

Guns, Gold and Caravans
China Caravans

AUTOBIOGRAPHY

Life and Work (with David Russell)
Love and War: Pearl Harbor Through V-J Day (with Jane Easton)

EDITINGS

Max Brand's Best Stories
Bullying the Moqui: Charles F. Lummis' Defense of the Hopi (with Mackenzie Brown)
Max Brand's Best Poems (with Jane Easton)
Max Brand: Collected Stories (with Jane Easton)

50th Anniversary Edition

The HAPPY MAN

A NOVEL OF CALIFORNIA RANCH LIFE

ROBERT EASTON

Foreword by GERALD W. HASLAM

Introduction by JACK SCHAEFER

CAPRA WESTERN CLASSICS SERIES

CAPRA PRESS
SANTA BARBARA

TO FREDERICK FAUST

Printed in the United States of America.

The Viking Press edition, 1943.
University of New Mexico Press edition, 1977.
Capra Press edition, 1993.

Cover painting by J. O'H. Cosgrave, II, from the original Viking edition. Four sections of *The Happy Man,*" Dynamite's Day Off," "Women and Dynamite," "The Wind of Pelican Island," and "The Happy Man" appeared in *The Atlantic Monthly*

LIBRARY OF CONGRESS CATALOGING-IN-PUBLICATION DATA
Easton, Robert Olney.
The happy man / Robert Easton.
p. cm.
ISBN 0-88496-340-3 : $12.95
1. Ranch life--California--Fiction. I. Title
PS3509.A7575H36 1993
813'.52--dc20
92-46339
CIP

CAPRA PRESS
POST OFFICE BOX 2068
SANTA BARBARA, CA 93120

FOREWORD

WHY DO CERTAIN books endure while others—even those more ballyhooed—fade? There's no pat answer for that, but one response is that once the frosting of promotion is scraped clear by readers, the quality of the work must be strong and its theme must contain at least some elements of universality.

1943 was dominated by books dealing with World War II, that terrible reality all had to face—John Hersey's *Into the Valley*, Ernie Pyle's *Here is Your War*, and Richard Tregaskis's *Guadalcanal Diary* among many memorable titles. But there were other successful novels that year: Betty Smith's *A Tree Grows in Brooklyn* remains memorable.

The surprise in 1943, however, was *The Happy Man*, a first novel by Robert Easton, a young Californian who was by then a soldier. Although it was not propelled by great hoopla, we're still reading it fifty years later. Easton's novel defied the Golden State's stereotype: no movie stars, no champagne cocktails or dashing playboys, just ranch hands and ranch life and human emotions—a glimpse of his native state's reality. The story was true and dramatic in its own right, while at the same time touching readers who knew nothing of the setting.

Observed the renowned Stephen Vincent Benét following *The Happy Man's* publication, "All I know about Robert Easton comes from the publisher's blurb. . . But, wherever he comes from, he is an addition to American letters, and you had better start collecting his first editions now." Fifty years later, it might be a good time to start collecting second and third editions too.

—GERALD W. HASLAM

INTRODUCTION

I have known Bob Easton for a good many years and this book, which led me to him, for even more years. I have reread it at various times through those years and each time, as my own experience and understanding have increased, my admiration for it has deepened. It has a timeless enduring quality. I have loaned my copy to half a dozen or more knowledgeable experts in western writing and invariably their verdicts have matched mine. It is a one-of-a-kind book, not derivative in any way, completely itself, the work of a young writer who had the stubbornness and great good sense to ignore the literary fashions and mannerisms of the period and to write his book in his way—and thus to create one of the authentic classics of the American west.

* * *

A happy set of circumstances combined for the writing of *The Happy Man*.

Robert Olney Easton was born in San Francisco on the Fourth of July, 1915. Twenty-five years later he went to work for the B.B. Cattle Company at

Collinsville, on the Sacramento Delta, where the Sacramento and San Joaquin rivers meet to form the head of San Francisco Bay. The years between had shaped a young American who was still an unregenerate westerner in heart and mind but one toned and tempered by eastern education.

His early years, well into his teens, were spent in the Santa Maria area of south-central California, with weekend and summer activity at Sisquoc Ranch, a historic land-grant cattle spread managed by his father. California schools were not then what they may be now; when he graduated from high school at sixteen he found himself poorly prepared for college. That was remedied by a school year across the continent at Phillips Academy in Andover, Massachusetts. Home again, he enrolled at Stanford University—and, dissatisfied again, jumped the continent once more to immerse himself in Harvard University and emerge three and a half years later with an A.B. degree. Harvard had put its imprint on him and he, as chairman of the board of editors of the *Lampoon,* had put his imprint on Harvard, at least in a mild way. Meanwhile he had also gone farther afield; he used a summer vacation for a tour through much of Europe, even traveling deep into Stalin's Russia, an experience which confirmed his faith in his own country and his boyhood conviction that his own true homeland was the Coast Range region of California.

Back home once again, Harvard behind him, he became associate editor of *Coast,* a regional journal published in San Francisco, and a few months later moved to Los Angeles to cover the southern portion of the state for the magazine. There he did editorial work and wrote feature articles, meeting all manner of interesting people—among them Jane Faust, daughter of Frederick Faust, the man known to millions of readers of westerns and other stories as Max Brand.

In 1940, *Coast* magazine collapsed and its associate editor was without a job. But he knew now what he wanted to do. He wanted to marry Jane Faust, and he wanted to become a cattleman and combine this with writing. In a matter of months he and Jane were married and he was a ranch hand with A. B. Miller's B.B. Cattle Company, the biggest feedlot operation in the west.

This new job was really new for him, far different from the range cattle work he had known at the Sisquoc, where the methods and traditions of the Spanish land-grant days still lingered. The B.B. was a huge beef manufactory, a vast largely mechanized business enterprise growing and processing its own feed, taking in scrawny cattle from here and there and everywhere by the trainload and the bargeload, turning them out sleek and fat and ready for the slaughterhouse.

The other men working there were new for him

too. Most of them were Okies and Arkansawyers who had known the bitterness of the grapes of wrath in their home territories during the depression and dust-bowl years of the 1930s. Young Bob Easton, working shoulder to shoulder with them, saw and truly understood them—as John Steinbeck had seen and understood others of them only a few years earlier. And again, like another Harvard man who had stepped off a train in Wyoming years before to meet a Virginian, he knew that a vital segment of his own education was just beginning.

Oh, yes, the B.B. Cattle Company was big business, a modern—very modern—business institution, no "ranch" in any real meaning of the word. But the Old West, the West of the wide open spaces and the men who ran cattle in them, was there too. It was there, unconscious and unformulated, in the minds and muscles of these men whose memories ran back to other times and other ways. They worked ten hours a day, seven days a week, when cattle shipments arrived late into the night and started again in earliest morning. The regular wage, never with any overtime, was three dollars a day—with a third of that taken out for board and bunk. They worked for that meagre money, yes, but they worked more out of loyalty to each other and to an outfit they respected and for the satisfaction of being part of a challenging enterprise and doing difficult work well. And always an emergency could, and would, arise when trucks and tractors and steel-muscled cranes were useless and they would have to rely on their own strengths and ingenuity and even at times swing into saddles and unleash loops as in the old days.

There on the Sacramento Delta vital material was being daily created for a young writer with open eyes and ears and mind. Bob Easton squeezed out moments to jot down notes. After about a year he had a fair supply—but there was no time for actual writing. In mid 1941 he changed jobs, going to work for the McCreery Ranch high in the Coast Ranges near Hollister. Better pay, better hours, more experience. He was on his way toward becoming a cattleman and combining this with writing. He was high in the heartland of the country he loved. He had a batch of basic material, his because he had lived it, been a part of it. And he had a successful veteran writer father-in-law who steadily and generously encouraged him.

Several possible chapters were down on paper and the book as a whole was taking shape in his mind. And on December 7 the Japanese bombed Pearl Harbor.

* * *

Inevitably, Bob Easton decided to volunteer for military service. Just as inevitably he aimed at enlistment as a cavalryman. What he discovered, traveling from post to post in search of a mounted unit, was that mechanization was taking over the armed forces as it had the production of beef at the B.B. He had to forgo the cavalry and enlist in the regular army—and his writing went right along with him. On through the months in training camps, usually on Sundays, he would perch in the rec hall on a chair, working at a little portable typewriter on another chair, ignoring the clatter and confusion around him. By the time the book was as finished as it ever would be—and many of us wish there were more of it—he was in training to become an officer with a tank destroyer battalion.

Along the way, in 1942, four chapters were published in the *Atlantic Monthly,* marked as "Atlantic firsts," the work of a new and competent writer. Early in 1943 the book itself was issued by the Viking Press.

* * *

Not many books, particularly first books by previously unknown writers, have been as well received by the reviewers as was *The Happy Man.* Top-rank critics for the country's major newspapers were positively enthusiastic about it. However boggled some of them were by the question of whether it was a novel or simply a series of related stories, they were virtually unanimous in praise. The general verdict was neatly summed by Stephen Vincent Benét in the course of a surprisingly full-scale commentary in the *New York Herald Tri-*

bune. These stories, he wrote, "are the best new stories in a long, long time." They are "just as much Mr. Easton's stories as Mr. Faulkner's are Mr. Faulkner's stories or Mr. Hemingway's are Mr. Hemingway's stories."

What the reviewers had recognized at once was that they had in hand the work of an authentic original talent. That the form of the book defied customary categories did not matter, because, as George R. Stewart noted in the *New York Times,* it had "what is necessary–quick narrative, infallible regional feeling, and a not often approached rendition of the vernacular."

Those are assets which show up plainly even in a quick reading and are rewarding enough in themselves. But what strikes one who comes really to know this book is that it stands firm through the years as a distinct literary achievement, a book with subtle overtones emerging out of the straightforward simplicity of narration, a book whose writer sought honestly to put down truthfully what he saw and heard, and did so–and in the doing, with never an obtrusive flourish of explanation or sentiment or stylistic trick, managed to convey his own deep bedrock feelings about it.

There is a richness of texture here, too, a satisfying wholeness despite the relative slimness of the book and its loose episodic structure. Everything needed for a full mental grasp on the life history from birth to dissolution of T. S. Ordway's El Dorado cattle empire and on the lives of the men who were part of it (and their women, too) is here, deftly woven, with no slackening of pace, into the narration. Moreover, the land and the waters and the wind and the weather are as vividly present and as vital to the telling as are the human characters themselves.

Stephen Vincent Benet had it right. Robert Easton, he wrote, "is an addition to American letters, and you had better start collecting his first editions now."

But after *The Happy Man* there were no more first editions to collect for a long, long time.

* * *

A world war had not blocked the writing or marred the critical reception of *The Happy Man,* yet in one sense the book became something of a war casualty. Those were the years of paper shortages and limited printings and public attention focused on battlegrounds across the oceans. Within a year selected chapters were being reprinted in anthologies whose editors understood their value, but in overall terms of general circulation the book, like many another of those war years, did not achieve the wide readership it merited. A contributing cause was that no books followed to keep the author and his work fresh in the public mind.

It is my belief that Bob Easton, as a writer, was

something of a war casualty too. Inevitably I think of this in terms of the title chapter of *The Happy Man,* which was one of those "Atlantic firsts" under the title "The Happiest Man." Why was that man happy? "He'd pitched his camp in the country he liked best—and never had to break it up." Bob Easton had pitched his camp in the country of the mind as well as geography he liked best—and the war made him break it up.

Four full years he was in uniform, more than two years of that in various European war areas, first with his tank destroyer battalion, then as a first lieutenant in the infantry. No doubt he lived those war years as intensely as he had his year with the B.B. Cattle Company—but his feelings about it all were certainly not the same. Moreover, when honorably discharged, he already had more family to consider and to support. Two children had been added, and another would be soon, and, before long, yet another. And Max Brand, who had encouraged him in his earlier maverick ways, had been killed in the war. That was, quite likely, the final wrench that completed the breakup of his happy man camp.

Oh, on through the postwar years he went on writing, along with other work, but more as an able all-around journeyman, not the master craftsman of that first book. He edited a small newspaper and managed a radio station in Lampasas, Texas, a town he had come to know well during military training. He wrote occasional short stories and articles for various popular magazines. He moved to Santa Barbara, close again physically at least to his onetime campsite, picked up a master's degree at the university there, and taught English in the local community college. He did technical writing as a consultant with the U.S. Naval Civil Engineering Laboratory at Port Hueneme. It was not until 1961, eighteen years after the publication of *The Happy Man,* that he published another book. This was a biography of Buffalo Jones written in collaboration with a longtime friend, Mackenzie Brown.

To me, that book about a buffalo hunter who spent his last years helping to save the last of the animals he had hunted indicates that Bob Easton was changing direction in his writing once again, moving back ever closer in his mind to the deep feeling for the land, for nature in its wholeness including man, which had come through in *The Happy Man.* During the next years he became ever more closely involved in conservation movements, leading in the fight to establish a sanctuary for California's condors and writing superbly about them, serving as chairman in the sustained battle to preserve Santa Barbara as a decent habitat for humans and as a trustee of Santa Barbara's Trust for Historic Preservation and its Museum of Natural History, standing up tall in indignation at the

Santa Barbara oil spill and doing amazing research on the whole subject of oil spills to produce *Black Tide,* a book that is already a classic in its own field.

But there has not yet been another "happy man."

The chance remains that there will be. Easton has slackened off some in the almost day-to-day conservation work that has been monopolizing his time, and he is hearkening back to the years of his boyhood and the Sisquoc Ranch and the B.B. Cattle Company and the McCreery Ranch—and always the land, the long history of the land, the Coast Range country he has always liked best. In his mind and in writing now under way he is pitching his camp there once more. He is hearkening back to his beginnings as a writer. I for one will want to learn what the years have done to his vision of this California country and a happy man.

It is an appropriate time for renewed publication of "the best new stories in a long, long time."

JACK SCHAEFER
Santa Barbara, California
1977

PUBLISHER'S NOTE: Jack Schaefer's hopes are being fulfilled in Robert Easton's Saga of California® series of historical novels, *This Promised Land, Power and Glory* and the forthcoming *Blood and Money.*

CONTENTS

PROLOGUE

THE year he died, Thomas S. Ordway told this story: As a child he was playing alone in the backyard and all at once the ground looked marvelously good, warm in the sunlight with the markings of his toys, so good you could smell it. And he stared until he knew that in all the world there was nothing real but himself and this ground running away across the yard and under the chicken coops and green back fence, across the alley and so on around the world. It put a tingle in his spine. He grabbed a fistful and rushed indoors where his mother was peeling carrots at the kitchen sink. "Gee, Ma," he cried, "I love this stuff!" holding up to her his tiny fist.

Not many years later Thomas Ordway crossed the Alleghenies and came West.

At twenty-one, within range of the breeze that

touches the coast of California every afternoon promptly, as though released by a certain position of the sun, he was farming five thousand acres in his own name—a young man lean and brown, good with his hands. He dressed in blue denim and shirt of hickory gray and wore a hat flared back the way the Rough Riders wore them in the war with Spain, as though young Tom were going places in a high wind.

He had ideas under that hat. His account grew. He got acquainted with the bankers and they picked him as a good man to back. Ordway did a little banking himself, learned how to rent a piece of ground and borrow on next year's sack of barley. He bought good clothes and was seen at the Palace Hotel. Gossips at the clubs he joined but had no time to patronize, described him as a "comer," not a "pusher"; and three years later when T. S. went South and cleaned up in oil by cornering options and selling before the bubble broke, they said he was a really smooth operator, a natural-born oilman, yessir.

Ten years later Ordway developed a big tract of land at the foot of the Alkali Mountains, what formerly was an out-wash plain of whitish dirt that hurt the eyes with its reflection and was of interest only to geologists who saw there features of the Miocene Era. Ordway saw what could be done with a little water dammed during the rainy season in upland canyons, a few wells bored. So he moved in, buying cheaply, developing, sold out what he had done and went North, leaving green five-acre farms where a small man could live easily with his orange trees and raise a few rabbits. Just another real estate deal. Or was it more? In those days Ordway never asked himself questions. He was too busy growing.

He did not marry. They said of Thomas Ordway that he loved children and trees, but it was land he loved the best. One day north by the river, he stood above the marsh alone, on a neck of land running among the sloughs, and saw the delta heaving in the afternoon wind like the green swell of the sea. Then the feeling took him—a sharp tingle of the spine, a promise and delight—that here was a chance, a big country not being used, with money in it.

Cannily the eye of Ordway got the scheme down on paper, observing means of entrance and exit, drainage, the prevailing wind, some marginal farms of Swiss dairymen half under water that would sell for the asking—all balanced and assessed. He stooped and let a handful of black earth sift through his fingers. Washing would cure the alkali—ditches, pumps, another fifty thousand.

Ordway decided; and because he never had stopped but gone on, he built here in the mud flats first the grain fields, then the wide city of boards and cattle, his feed-yard. Now in middle age he had been taken by the desire for a completed product—something to represent the cycle of living things he knew—beginning with the land, through grain, to flesh made from the grain, which naturally suggested cattle. The idea was pleasingly simple. Men had followed it in a small way since the time of Genghis Khan, and earlier, but never in the manner of Thomas Ordway.

Between the golden inland valleys and the coastal cities the river carried his freight cheaply. The railroads came. When help was needed, he hired it at the market price; and then, whether he realized or not, the life of Thomas Ordway became a hundred times more important because mingled with it and depending on it were the lives of all the people who worked for him and lived by what he decided.

Then it was time for a story. Given the place and the people, a story follows. Yet for all that has been said, the story is not so much about Thomas Ordway as about the life he created, that contained him, and the land he used in his turn. Most of the evidence is documentary and can speak for itself.

TO FIND A PLACE

On a Saturday morning in September a man drove a small out-of-date coupé along a county road bordering some yellow California hills. The road humped slightly every so often where the slopes had washed and fanned off into a long plain, flat as a pan, that ran away westward toward salt marshes and a bay. The name of the man doesn't matter—call him "I" if you like. But he was young, a stranger in these parts, and looking for his first job.

It was a few minutes before one o'clock when I caught the scent of many animals, mixed with the pleasant and exciting smell of sea wind over the summer ground, and topped the last hump in the road and saw the feed-yards of the El Dorado Investment Company, and all its thirteen thousand white-faced cattle cooped in pens like city blocks that spread away for miles clear to the river and the yellow fields bordering it.

At a sign with a great hand pointing, I turned and drove to a small box of a building that said: OFFICE, and here I inquired of a sleepy bookkeeper when Mr. Archibald Jacks, the foreman, could be expected. The answer was one o'clock, at the barn, and the barn was over there two hundred yards where all the cattle began.

While the bookkeeper was talking, I let my eye wander a little—since this was the office of the largest enterprise of its kind in western America, I wanted to have a look—and on the panel of an inner door I saw "T. S. Ordway, Private." I thought about it as I drove away. T. S. Ordway was a name known to most people west of the Rockies. He didn't raise cattle; he manufactured them. He turned beef into dollars as fast as Henry Ford turned cars off the assembly line. Three months in his yards and the heifer yearlings that had come so poor, so cheap, were shipped away as sleek as seals with half their added pounds clear profit. And he had steers, too, and canner cows and baloney bulls and anything that wore horns and a hide. He didn't care. "Give me the cattle ninety days," he used to say, "and I'll not have to brand 'em. They'll take the look o' the El." By which he meant his brand was the Rocking EL and his cattle stuffed so hard with good white fat that butchers who knew never bothered coming to see the animals they wanted; they simply telephoned and said, "Tom, I need a load of heifers to average eight-seventy-five," just as you would order so many pairs of shoes from a catalogue.

So I went along into that wilderness of boards and cattle where everything was strange, and stopped, and left the car and stood beside a fence not too near the door of the barn nor yet too far away, but just between—about the place I thought correct for a young man who didn't have a job but hoped to get one.

Trucks were going by—big semi-trailers full of hay, partitioned in the middle like orange boxes. They sang past me down the road and I saw the flash of the sun-and-wind-burned faces with whom I was to work; and my own face got red and my clothes didn't fit and the chromium on my old coupé, which I had taken such scrupulous care of these past five years, looked as bright and silly as French doors on a barn. Trucks and more trucks passed, flat-beds, Diesels—every kind, in pairs, in convoys disappearing toward some secret destination in the heart of Thomas Ordway's city, where the warehouses and mill rose like castles of galvanized iron, and a gigantic pit for beet-pulp, wide as a stadium, filled the air with a sour, sticky smell. An arm of the river, a man-made slough, reached in here, and barges were tied close against a dock and giant cranes moved over them, nodding and whirling as they bit and lifted and spat away the pulp to empty the barges and fill the pit.

From everywhere there rose the sounds of action—of belts and wheels, frictions, grindings, loadings and liftings and all the business of a morning—till even the air you breathed was busy and I could see the sweat of working men soak through their shirts between the shoulder blades. Still no foreman came. If anyone had handed me a hoe and said: "Here, go to work!" I would have considered myself far richer than T. S. Ordway.

About then somebody did come, a man in a dusty pick-up who stopped his little truck five steps away and slumped immediately behind the wheel and began picking his teeth with a match. He had a short face, brown and wrinkled as a nut, sharp as a rodent's, and he wore an ancient cattleman's hat. He stuck both thumbs under the bib of his overalls and stared at the horizon while the match worked itself across his mouth and back again.

"You Mr. Jacks?" I asked.

"Part of the time," said the man, looking far away. His attention veered slightly to the southwest. He began singing in a flat nasal voice: "O Susanna, don't you cry for me . . ." but broke off suddenly and said, looking due south, "You the new man?"

I said I was.

Archibald Jacks hummed another bar.

"They's-a-boy-inside-the-barn-'ll-show-ye-what-to-do," he popped out all together and at the same time was stricken into action, dropped his song, spat out his match, started his pick-up, and drove away.

In the doorway of the barn I met a little man all in blue denim, so bowlegged you could have put a half-grown hog between his knees and never got his blue jeans dirty.

"Howdy," said the little man. He led a saddled horse and he leveled at me a pair of eyes like two revolvers.

I said "Howdy" quickly, the first time I remember ever using the word, and somehow it sounded like an echo to "Hands-up!"

Yet the little man was not unfriendly. He had heard of me; he would show me my horse. "Barb's a gentle horse," he said, leading the way down the barn, behind the mangers. "Pretty good cowhorse, too, for this part of the country." He pointed to a chunky sorrel with white stockings. "Looks more like the ponies we had back home."

"Where was that?" I asked.

"Utah," said the little man. "Guess Utah was the last one I had. Say, what do they call you?"

I told him my name and the little man put his hand out and said, "Mine's Dynamite."

"Danny?" I said.

"No," he said, quite seriously, "*Dynamite.*" He was adjusting a stirrup for me. "Never did give a damn for twisted stirrup leathers," he said. "Never did see 'em till I come to Californy. Or Oregon. Guess Oregon was first. . . . I'd rode for this feller quite some time, Charlie Devers, Ringbolt Charlie, we called him. I'd noticed once before his leathers was twisted but I just figured, you know, that they'd *got* twisted and he'd straighten 'em when he had the chance. So one day we was riding for White River to do something—I forget what just now, to see a feller who had horses or something. . . . Anyhow, we'd got us down the road a spell and broke our ponies to a lope and I noticed them leathers o' Charlie's still was twisted. 'Hey,' I hollers, 'your leathers!' Charlie, he cranes first over this side, then over that, and looks and gets darker in the face with looking, till I knowed his thunder was a-gonner roll. 'Twisted?' he says. 'Boy, *you're* telling *me* them leathers is twisted? Now what the hell is the matter with you? How do you think leathers orter be?' Oh, he'd got kindy flusterated, took him clear to White River to cool out; and then I explained how back home all the leathers was hung straight. See, he'd never heard o' my way and I'd never heard of his'n, but I guess that's the way it is in life—they's a heap of things a feller never hears about till he travels and meets other folk but his own."

Dynamite made a little boy's grin. He had animal teeth, very white and sharp. "That's how you'll be here," he said, slapping the rump of Barb, the chunky sorrel, "meetin' other folk but your own. So let's start now and get acquainted."

He led the way outside.

Dynamite rode a ragged bay that was the very meaning of the word nag, all head and hind-end, and when he was aboard he showed me how his stirrups hung freely so that he could rake a bronc with his spurs from its ears to its hips. Then he took off down an asphalt road, where Barb and I got just three feet of clearance from the whining trucks, like any other vehicle, and finally we turned into a side alley between mangers lined with cattle, where the feeding heads made a solid row of white almost within touching of my stirrup. The Herefords hardly raised an eye to watch us pass. This, said Dynamite, was because a feed-truck had just dumped its load. He said ten of them took all day to feed the yards, that each lot of cattle was given a number and a pen when it came in, and thereafter was never moved until ready to cut and ship, that a good heifer might gain three pounds a day while a steer put on two, but she-stuff brought a cent less per pound because they had more waste to them. "Take these ladies here, 364's; we're shipping on 'em now. See that roan by the water trough, how the fat fits tight along her back and covers her hip bones and makes them like pads aside her tail? See that satchel down in front between her legs? That's what you eat when you eat boiled brisket. . . . Now lookie her alongside these here ones over here, 369's; they just come in last week. Both are long yearlings, both good Hereford, but these on this side is just a-commencin' to eat. See the bellies on 'em? If a critter don't belly-down thataway first, she won't never get fat."

Dynamite pointed out the different brands, all famous through the West, the Open-A-Bar, the SQ, Double Slash, and 3C—each speaking for a country and a people like the flags of ships met in a harbor. One came from Stovepipe out of Amarillo, one from west Texas, one from Oklahoma prairie and the plains of Oregon. Each stood for its great name—Pecos, Rio Grande, Houston, and Tombstone—for running irons, dust and leather, and range fires by the rim-rock. "They'd take a lot of tellin', them brands," said Dynamite, "but to make it easy old T. S. Ordway put 'em in a pen and just called 'em 369's."

The cattle ate an evil-smelling mash that had something like gold dust scattered over it. I asked what this might be and Dynamite said the mash was pulp left from the processing of sugar beets and the dust was dry-feed from the El Dorado's mill, where oat and barley hay were chopped with vetch and alfalfa and mixed with grain and milo maize, cottonseed cake, molasses, bone meal rich in phosphorous, and one or two other ingredients that made the best meal a cow critter ever ate and that laid the fat on thick and hard and white as cream. The exact proportion only T. S. Ordway knew. It was his discovery, his secret, and on it he had built his El Dorado. "He ain't no cattleman, hell . . . he's a businessman. Why, all of this place ain't no more than a drawer in his desk. He owns ranches from here to Mexico, banks, buildings in Los Angeles and San Francisco—everything a man can own. But he knows land best. It was land brought him here." Dynamite swept the western horizon with his arm. "Twenty thousand acres of the richest land in America. Sure, it was under water, half of it, when he come. Give him credit. He done her, he made her, and she's all his."

I looked into the wind that filled my eyes with Thomas Ordway's golden feed, whipped from the mangers, and saw it coming on the yellow fields up from salt marshes and the bay.

"Some panoramic, eh?" said Dynamite.

In the sunlight the sloughs wound through the reeds like threads of silver. Gulls and water-birds were dark motes floating high, shining white suddenly when they tipped against the sun. Beyond them the river spread to make a bay and far in the distance was again compressed by hills. I let my eye follow the compass round. South across the water was a fringe of little towns so far away their houses looked like pebbles on the opposite shore. Eastward along the yards low harvest hills unfolded to the river, with here and there a flock of sheep like a cluster of gray aphids. Northward for many miles the great alluvial plain rose gradually until it met the hills from which it had come; and, everywhere beyond, more hills rolled northward as far as a man might see, holding in their hollows clumps of unpainted farm buildings that looked as if they were dying there slowly, like bits of wood in the trough of the sea. And all of these hills were such a color of gold and had in them such a marvelous grace of line that when you looked steadily they seemed to move, as though they might have flowed once from the same source and instantly been stilled.

"She's big, is El Dorado," said Dynamite, "and

famous; but she has her faults like the rest of us. Some things you'll like, some not. Jacks, he's a good boss; the work ain't hard; the fellers of the best. But you'll wonder at seven working days a week and nights when they need you to unload cattle, and three bucks for a day. But we have a good time. We got to. . . . You will, too, when you're 'quainted around. Go up to Bird Town payday, come to our dances— Say, we're having one tonight and you can come. Ever square-dance? All we need's a fiddle and a bare floor, none o' this here fox-trot shilly-shally."

A truck that looked like a cigar box high on a frame was coming down the alley spewing beet-pulp out one side and leaving just enough room for a very thin horse to pass if he had steady nerves. Perched on a rear platform was a man who regulated the speed of unloading and called to the cattle in the pens who followed him bucking and bawling with delight. I followed Dynamite and threw my reins away, let old Barb take me past the truck with nearly an inch to spare between my right knee and the steel frame. Dynamite was already in conversation with the man on the rear platform whose name was Whitey and who, all the time he talked, was kicking a lever with his foot and poking at the pulp with a big feed-fork and interrupting himself now and then to cry out something in a high voice nobody could understand but which meant that the driver was to move on. Dynamite and I came slowly behind.

"Goin' to the dance?"

"Shore 'nuff."

"You wasn't to the last one."

"Shore was."

"Like hell."

"*Shore* I was; I'd go to a dance even if there was nobody there but me."

"I can believe it."

"No, I didn't go. Did you?"

"Yeah."

"How come?"

"Well, I figured you wasn't a-gonna be there."

"Oh, scairt, eh?"

And so it went for a hundred yards down the alley, until the pulp was all gone into the manger and Whitey gave a final cry and a wave to us and was whisked away for another load.

Whitey talked funny—not straight Western like Dynamite nor fully Southern, but something in between. For instance, he pronounced "wrench" and "ranch" exactly alike.

I asked where fellows came from who talked like that.

"Arkansas," said Dynamite. "Ain't you never heard a Arkansawyer talk? Well, you will. That's what we got here, along with the Okies and Missourians, and some from Texas. But you can tell a Arkansawyer. Mostly he's long and thin, red-cheeked and full of big old lies. Great hands to talk, they are, and to throw stones, and every one that's rode a horse says he's a cowboy. Like Jacks—he's one; but he ain't no cowboy. He's just a Arkansas farm boy growed up into a good job, and fat cattle is all he knows. Okies, they's different. We ain't got many that's gen-u-ine but one bunch lives up to Bird Town that I'll show ye, a whole county of 'em, Grandad, old Mammy, Pap and Ma, married boys and their kids—all junked together in one room. You couldn't miss 'em. They all got long manes and that drawed-up look, and wear them Okie caps like they was a-gonna drive a train some place."

I said California people didn't care much for Okies. "There's been a lot of hard words said about them and a lot written."

"Well," said Dynamite, "I tell you . . . I-tell-you-how-it-is. Take a sack of beans out of the field—any kind, pink, white, no matter—and pour 'em in a kettle and see how the foul stuff always comes on top—the straws and little stones. Same way with people. Pour your state into mine and it's the foul stuff shows up most, but the good beans is underneath there just the same, only a feller don't see 'em right away. Shucks sakes, we all got poor white trash—Utah, California, New York City—all of us. 'T ain't nothing to git flusterated over. . . . These folk here, they's good beans, not trash. Maybe they had a place back home but the dust got it, or maybe they got brothers and sisters'n enough back there to care for the old folks and they has to git out and rustle for theirselves. . . . Sure," said Dynamite, and then his eye wandered quickly and he shouted, "Hey you, Will Ragan, what kind of janitor's work are ye up to this day?"

A man bending over a water-trough in one of the pens straightened up slowly and revealed a shaggy Irish face on which three days' growth of beard lay like a heavy frost. "The work o' lazy cowboys is what I'm up to this day," said William Ragan, folding his hands across the top of a broom he had been using to clean the trough and getting ready to enjoy himself.

"Now lookie here, lookie here! . . . I'll not have no talkin' smart on such a day!" said Dynamite, and they both laughed and laughed. "Say, what did ye think of the fight?" Dynamite meant the prizefight of the night before in which a Pittsburgh Irishman had nearly whipped Joe Louis.

"Oh, aye," said William, "and it's well enough, I guess. Or else the Irish would be a-thinkin' themselves better than the niggers." And again he roared and slapped his thigh and poked Dynamite's horse in the flank with his broom handle, and there was three minutes' general rampage before Dynamite and I could go on.

We passed a construction crew repairing an alley, and Dynamite got his little boy's grin ready for each man and a word launched with the full vigor of his name: "Hi Fred, hi Jingle. . . . Not doin' much, eh, Joe?" And to a man named Tex leaning on a shovel: "*Care*-ful! Easy there, Tex, or ye're a-gonner bust that handle!" He called them all the WPA and cursed them, and they loved it.

Then for a while Dynamite had nothing to say, so he sang a song:

O send me a letter,
Send it by mail.
Send it in care *of*
The Birmingham jail.
The Birmingham jail, love.
The Birmingham jail. . . .
The Birmingham jail. . . .
Pining for you, love. . . .

On a space of level ground we passed a haystack three hundred feet long and thirty high where a crane unloaded semi-trailers of hay. The trucks drove alongside the stack; the crane swung over, dangling a cable to which the driver hooked both ends of a net made of wire that lined the compartments of the truck and onto which the hay had been loaded. Five seconds later a parcel weighing several tons was delivered on the stack just as freight is loaded on a ship, there to be spread around by three men with pitchforks. "Old Ordway figured it," said Dynamite. "They tell how he come down here one afternoon and seen a dozen guys pitching hay and a dozen more trying to catch what the wind didn't blow away, and then he set and went to thinkin' and next Tuesday-week he bought the Company another crane and a hundred yards of wire cable and let a dozen men go down the road."

So we made our rounds until we came to the scalehouse by the mill where the men like to sit for a smoke in the shade, or go inside the little iron shack and read the *True Detectives* Gene, the weighmaster, keeps piled there under his scale. By four o'clock it's time for talking; so the boys were ready on the bench when Dynamite and I came around. Then they shut up like clams and looked at the earth and the sky and somehow managed to see everything there was about me before I'd got within a hundred yards.

Dynamite sailed right in. "Jody," he said to a thin little man with glasses and a great big country hat of straw, "don't pay no 'tention to them other guys but just give me a plain answer: when do we run our race?"

"Any time suits me," said Jody, making marks on the ground with the used end of a match.

"Okay then," said Dynamite, "tomorry. We'll run tomorry instead of going to church. We'll measure out one hundred yards of the road this side o' Bird Town."

"You want to make a man work Sunday?" said Jody.

"*Chicken*!" said a young man who lounged out of the scalehouse and was able to keep both hands in his pockets by nudging the screen with one elbow and letting it slam shut behind. "Jody, he's made ye a play. Auntie or throw in your hand." Jaydee Jones, raised on Arkansas corn fritters, ham and hominy, had at one time or other taken something dark inside him that came out now on his face and made every word he said funny, with a sting. Not looking anywhere in particular, he sauntered over to Dynamite and began combing his horse's mane with the fingers of one hand. He asked if there was a dance that night, if Lear had paid Dynamite the two bucks. Then Jaydee's face got serious with thought. "Say," he said, "did you hear about that 'lectrician over at Vista City?"

"What about him?" said Dynamite.

"Dead," said Jaydee.

"Yeah?" said Dynamite.

For a minute, then another minute and another that was all.

"How did it happen?" I asked.

Jaydee said quickly, "Oh, he set down on a fruit cake and a currant ran up his laig."

The only sound was a muffled rubbing of the gears inside the mill. Jaydee sauntered back and leaned against the wall of the scalehouse and called for somebody inside named Pringle to bring him out the Climax Plug.

"Well," Dynamite said to me, "the hell with these guys. We got important business to attend to. Let's get outta here."

We rode away and when I saw Dynamite watching me, I grinned for the little cowboy and said, "I was cut too green, wasn't I? Bet if you'd stick me in the ground, I'd grow."

"Aw shucks," said Dynamite. "You ate horse, sure. But we all got to sometimes. Now you'll know Jaydee—he's kindy thataway."

We rode the alley toward the barn, watching for leaky troughs or boards off gates, dead animals, or any of those casual changes the laws of chance occurrence bring wherever a species is gathered. We found only Jacks, sitting in his pick-up by the barn as though he just happened to be there, sucking a match and looking at the horizon. In a voice so confidential it would have served to announce the merger of six companies he told Dynamite the cattle trucks would be in at eleven.

When he had gone, Dynamite swore all around the compass. "Never knew it to fail, *never* did. Cattle, cattle every day in the week and if a feller wants to dance Saturday night and have a little fun, it's nothing doing, it's *cattle.* Jesus Christ. I quit."

He stormed into the barn.

He was still saying "To hell with 'em; I quit," when the ponies were bedded-down and I was driving toward the buildings of the main ranch. "Lemme out here," said Dynamite as we passed a quadrangle of galvanized iron garages, the place the feed-trucks stayed all night.

"You're not going to the bunkhouse?" I asked.

"Me? Hell no. What would I want with a bunkhouse. I got one o' my own up to Bird Town. Wife and four kids in it." Dynamite lifted himself out, then reached for his lunch-bucket. "I'll call for ye at eleven," he said, still angry, and walked away.

To reach the bunkhouse of the El Dorado Investment Company, you passed a kind of used-car lot where no vehicle built within the last ten years, with any paint, upholstery, unbroken window, or any kind of operating decency, was exhibited. The bunkhouse itself was two old farmhouses sewn together with some sketchy carpentering. There were in all about a dozen bare rooms—six beds in the front one and so on back. Over a kind of closet by the door someone had smeared "Bull Cook" in red paint. I knocked here and an old man came out and pointed to a bed in the corner beside what once had been a chiffonier. "Give the mattress a once-over," he said, handing me the fly-spray. "Wash-room's out back. The Widder Ellen, we call it, is that house by the cypress tree."

I worked over the mattress, then dumped my blankets on the bed and took a towel and went to find the wash-room. Men coming from work lined the sink. There were gray basins and hot and cold running water. In the confusion it was easy to come and go and I would have moved unnoticed but for the electrician who had sat upon the fruit cake. I read knowledge of this unhappy story in every face and fled away indoors, devoured by a thousand eyes. I spent the time till supper lying on my bed because there was no place to sit except a bench and table in the middle of the room, where a man might expect to sit when he had worked for the El Dorado at least a year and never asked questions out of turn.

The occupants of the other beds came in. You would find them repeated over and over in any bunkhouse of the West, men of indefinite age, the old Jaspers who drive the Chevies and Model-A Fords, who lift the picks and build the fences, whose only home is four bare walls and a bare floor.

The supper bell rang before it was time to light two bulbs that hung on cords from the ceiling. Nobody had said a word.

I followed behind the men, under cypress trees where the wind touched mournfully, into the cookhouse where all the others found seats. The long table was set with white oilcloth and heavy white plates and dishes heaping with food. Through an open door was the kitchen; the cook stood over his black stove, and rows of pots and spoons and knives hung each from its nail. In the doorway lounged a great gob of a man who wore a sailor's hat and nothing over his undershirt and pants but an apron. He smiled stupidly at everyone, his teeth protruding, and when I told him I was a new hand, said, "Sure, sure!" and laid one greasy paw across my back and pointed with the other to the end of the table.

There were boiled spuds and fat red beans that would keep a man going all day long, and pale string beans that really were strung, and also meat done country style, to the color and texture of gray leather. At intervals along the table stood those mysterious clumps of sauces, bottles that are never used or cleared away but stand forever fixed to the tables of American ranches—a sort of nucleus around which meals are built.

I carefully did not ask for things beyond my reach for fear of drawing attention, but the men were too busy to look at me. Along the table the double row of bodies bent and went to eating with a deadly earnest, hunched forward, no two alike yet all the same, each scarred and twisted, grown crooked from the roots, too long for its trunk or too short for its head, here missing a thumb, here an eye; yet all of them had grown in spite of every difficulty, like tough cedar trees from a rock.

Except for the Arkansawyers, the eaters were silent. But these were so altogether friendly they just couldn't stand to see a bite go down alone; it had to have a word for company, or maybe two. And if three were needed and your mouth was full of potatoes, that didn't matter—it just showed what a good man could do with the English language. "Jody," said Jaydee Jones, "pass me the Mussolini."

Jody handed over a platter of red spaghetti.

"You backed out today," said Jaydee. "Jody, you got feather-legged."

"Aw, you're just a-talkin' now," said Jody.

"Diney offered ye the chance; ye wouldn't run."

"Let's me and *you* run," said Jody.

"Me run again you? Why man," said Jaydee, "I'd tromp you to death in fifty yards."

"Let's make it a hundred then," said Jody. "I sure wanta live till payday."

"Hell, I run down a deer once't," went on Jaydee.

"That's nothing," Jody said. "Look at Roy there; he run down a Arkansas woman."

Everybody did look at Roy who got about the color of the spaghetti.

"Sure," said Jaydee, "and ever since he ain't been able to buy her a pair of shoes."

The fat waiter wanted to be friends. While everybody still was laughing at Roy, he called from the doorway to Jaydee, "Jaydee, hey Jaydee! . . . Let's you and me go to Sacramento this Saturday. I know a couple of dolls up there on G Street." Most of all the fat waiter wanted to be acquainted with a man named Sandy, who sat back-toward him on the near side of the table. Whenever possible, he stood close to Sandy, watching him dumbly like an affectionate dog. He brought freshly filled platters with "Here Sandy, try this. . . . Here Sandy, this'll put lead in your pencil." When Sandy talked about wild parties with the man next to him, the fat waiter eagerly broke in, "Did you ever throw a whing-ding in Chicago?" But Sandy kept on talking and after a while the waiter had to make his own answer, grinning at the air: "Boy, I sure did in '36. I *sure* threw a hummer there!"

After supper the men stacked their dishes and left them on the table by the kitchen door. Nobody smoked until he got outside and then within ten steps every man seemed to have rolled and lit a Bull Durham. They went in groups of three or four, laughing, swearing, tripping each other, ragging Jody about his foot-race and Roy about his Arkansas woman; and at intervals between them walked a solitary figure, a stranger, an habitual grouch, a pervert, a Mexican, or some other outcast—each desiring in his heart nothing so much as to be included in these rough words and coarse laughter.

Someone had switched the lights on in the bunkhouse and lit a fire in the wood stove. The bare bulbs brought to completion the bare walls, ceiling, floors, and faces of the men and made them into a little world of barrenness sealed by the night. They lay upon their beds, heads on folded hands, and stared at the ceiling until time to go to bed. Though it was hot and the place filled quickly with tobacco smoke, nobody opened a window. Nobody said a word.

I slept. The next I knew, Dynamite was standing over me, saying, "Come along, cowboy."

Outside it was bright starlight. The wind had risen and darkness had released into it ten thousand new and exciting smells, each like a thought of voyages and adventure, and now it rose again and beat above us wildly through the trees like water on a lonely shore.

Dynamite's car was a 1926 Packard Sedan, a monster-vehicle, the kind wealthy ladies keep forever in their retinue, pensioned like faithful servants. But here the lady died too soon. Dynamite paid seventy-five dollars for the car, he said, and told how it came in handy as nursery for his children and as a truck for hauling wood or hogs or calves that were born in the yards and taken home. It had no glass in the rear door, no rear seat, no upholstery that a child or a hog had not stained and scented permanently, but wonderful to say—and this Dynamite pointed out immediately—the vases inside the rear doors that once a liveried chauffeur had filled with jasmine and gardenias, were still unbroken, and in one of them were tucked brown shreds of flowers, poppies, placed there last spring by one of Dynamite's little girls.

Dynamite parked beside the barn, scrunched down and kicked his feet up on the dashboard, and told me to get in back if I liked, because the trucks might be an hour or they might be five. Reluctantly I did so, climbing over from the front seat into I-could-not-see-what perils, and finally making myself almost comfortable between an old tire and a wad of gunny sacks that served as rear seat.

For a time nothing was said. The wind brought a cold mist up from the marshes that shut out the stars and set the fog-horns moaning on the river. Across the road cattle stirred in their pens, coughing now and then, and the wind beside us made a lonely, lonely sound through the cracks in the barn.

"Oh, I hate this place!" said Dynamite. "Sometimes I hate it more than ever I did man or woman. Funny a feller can git so riled at just a place. But Jesus, seven days a week is wearisome, very wearisome. Last time I had off was in May to go to a rodeo—one day I took."

Again he was quiet; then flared up, "I and the wife had hell tonight. . . . Got home from work, nobody there, no bath, no supper, chickens into the tomatoes, back door open. Pretty soon, here they come, the whole dang chivaree and the dog, trailing in off the hill like a herd a-comin' to water. 'What the hell is it now?' I says to her. . . . I was mad anyway, see, 'bout not gettin' to the dance. Well, it was the sow. 'The sow *this*, the sow *that, the sow got restless so we let her out*. . . .' Well, the sow's gonna farrer, that's why she's restless, and I told that woman a thousand times not to let her out 'cause she'll hide her pigs sure as hell's fire, and we'll have fed her six months for nothing. So I was mad and we went round and round. Me and the wife don't get along, anyway. Never did."

"You're from Utah," I said. "I thought people there had lots of wives and were always happy."

"No more, they don't, least not in public; but I knew old Mormons back in the Bookcliffs that by God never knowed they'd joined the United States. They done her the old way still—wives, kids, the whole shebang. Oh, Mormons is good people. Take an outlaw traveling through their country—they'll always help him, never squeal on him."

"You're a Mormon?"

"Oh, kind of, I guess—kind of a Jack-Mormon. That was when I worked for one on Tennessee Crick out o' Rock City—old Josiah Bean. . . . Bear of a worker, old Joey was, and a devil of a good man with stallions. Had dozens of 'em. Some he'd caught wild out of the hills and some he'd raised, but they all was gentle when he come around. He taught me a lot about stallions. 'Never let 'em get away with nothin',' he says, 'A stallion's not like a gelding that'll try ye once and quit;

he's cocky. He figures if you win today, maybe he'll win tomorry, and he'll keep a-trying ye and keep a-trying.' I seen old Joey lead a black maverick stud through a barn full of mares, and if old stud cocked an ear or made so much as a whicker under his breath, Joey'd turn and just kick the stuffin' outa him right under the belly where it hurts, and then he'd turn around and lead that stud back and forth two or three times more just to show him. Great guy, old Joey. . . . Used to talk the Mormon religion to me. I was just a snot of a kid then and I guess he figured he'd get me early and lead me in the blessed way. I'd sit there on a bale of hay and let my eyes get big as saucers when he'd talk about God and Hellfire. . . . Pretend to take it all, you know, but Joey had a little daughter sixteen years old, Letticia, Letticia Bean, that I took to more'n ever I did his preaching. I never could go that stuff about turn yer other cheek when a guy slaps ye on this one. . . . Could you?"

I said I'd found it hard to go sometimes.

"And that stuff about Hellfire, how when a feller goes to Hell and gets to burnin' he don't never burn up, just stays there forever and burns and burns. I can't see it. I can't see how any Lord Jesus is gonna be that cruel. Why take even these here gangsters, John Dillingers and people, you wouldn't want to treat them that way, would ye? And tell *me* that just ordinary folks like you and me that does a sin or two is a-gonna burn and burn! *I* can't see it. . . .You got religion?"

"Kind of," I said. "My grandfather was a minister."

"Catholic?"

"No, Episcopal."

"A what?"

I explained about the Episcopal Church.

"My granddaddy was a Baptist," said Dynamite. "That's pretty near the same as a Christian, ain't it?"

I agreed and Dynamite continued: "I had an Aunt Olga that was great on the Catholic Church—what I mean she was for it strong! Used to say she'd give God Almighty anything she had and I reckon she would. Uncle Willie was different. He was off somewheres most of the time, though he always did send money home, and every year or two he'd come back himself and Olga would have another baby—nineteen she totaled. But she thought the world of Uncle Willie. Said she'd rather live with him in a dugout than with any other man in a castle, and that's about what she done. . . . Oh, that Uncle Willie was a great feller to hunt! One time I remember, he went to Canada and sent Aunt Olga home a moose, just the head of it, ye know. . . . Oh, I guess this here God-business is all right if ye like it, I just don't care for it myself."

I was sleeping again when Dynamite sang out, "Here they be!" and I heard the guttural roar of the Diesel and saw the dark hull of truck-and-trailer turning toward the barn, cutting the fog with powerful searchlights and decorated fore and aft like a ship with red and yellow clearance lights. The monster shifted gears and roared on by to find the chute.

Dynamite was there before it, signaling the driver with his flashlight as the door came opposite the chute. Then he took the bull-board, a small beam four feet long and several inches wide fitted with iron crosspieces at the end, and dropped it in the narrow gap between the chute and the truck. Then he undid and lifted out the door and wired it to the side of the chute. From inside came the stench of cattle. They were seen dimly, stowed like sacks in the darkness. They did not try to come out.

Dynamite climbed the top of the truck. The driver was standing by a headlight looking at his watch.

"Hey there below!" shouted Dynamite.

"Hey there above!" shouted the driver. "Is that you, Powder Keg?"

"And who else might it be, will ye tell me that? And while ye are at it, tell me where ye've been this past hour and a half?"

"Whadya mean 'Where have I been?' I been traveling, boy, traveling! Since eight o'clock this morning I've had my nose to that old concrete."

"Oh, don't hand me them stale pertaters. I know you guys—stop here for a steak, stop there for a beer, stop in Modesto to see my gal. . . ."

While he was talking, Dynamite kicked at the heads of the cattle nearest the door, and now he turned on them his full atention in words that lashed like cuts of rawhide. "Hyar, hyar ye sons of bitches! Outside!"

But the cattle were afraid of the open door.

"Shine your light in the chute," commanded Dynamite, and when this was done, the cattle went right out. They were small cattle, yearlings, poor and weak. "Where did ye get *these* things?" said Dynamite.

"Oh, down the line there five hundred miles. . . . Havermeyers, isn't it? I got it on my book. First trip ever I made to that place."

"Bad road?"

"Bad road! . . . No road at all. Blue cracked a drive shaft coming out and Dolly—no telling when Dolly'll be here."

"Never knew it to fail," said Dynamite.

The driver pulled ahead, the trailer was unloaded, and Dynamite and I took the cattle down the alley a hundred yards to the scales, Dynamite explaining that by order of the State Railroad Commission, which being a *railroad* commission naturally had it in for trucks, all cattle-trucks must weigh their loads immediately on reaching their destination, while for the railroads this was not true. "It's the old railroad graft, is what it is. They got their commission, see? And the trucks ain't got the chance of a snowball in hell."

The scales was a galvanized iron building at the end of the alley. You pushed the cattle clear down and then closed a gate which held them in the alley till you could go around and open the scale door and push the critters in, one draft at a time. Dynamite went ahead inside and lit an electric bulb, and I could hear him slapping the iron markers on the bar until they came in balance. "We'll take 'em half-and-half," the cowboy called, coming back, and we advanced together in the darkness and let the shapes of yearlings swirl around us toward the light until Dynamite leaped out, shouting terribly, which drove back half the bunch and sent the others nearly out the end of the scales. He slammed the heavy door just in time to stem the backwash of cattle and I followed him into the region of the electric bulb, which was nothing but a bare dirt floor and a box that housed the weighing mechanism and a board that jutted from the wall and evidently served as desk, for there were two old notebooks on it and a pencil.

"Ye can count 'em off," said Dynamite, bending over and tapping the markers and saying, "Whoa, cattle, whoa, cattle," in a voice designed to keep the tangled, swirling, bawling mass of cattle on the scale from destroying itself. I looked at the yearlings through a crack between two boards. The yellow light striped them weirdly. They didn't look at all poor or weak, and I wondered how any man on earth would be able to count them when that door came open.

"Okay!" sang Dynamite.

I opened the door wide.

Nothing happened. Then one animal put a foot out; then it took a step; then an avalanche of cattle rattled out over the boards like stones rolling down a mountain.

"How many?" said Dynamite.

"Dunno," I said.

"Didn't think ye would," said Dynamite. "But that's okay; that's all right. Next time stand out front a little and they'll not go so fast."

"Yeah, that's all right," I said. "That's hell, that's *suicide!*"

Dynamite laughed and laughed.

The truck had rolled down opposite the scales and stopped, its great cylinders idling hoarsely, getting their breath after five hundred miles. The driver, known as "Done Movin', the Laziest Man in the World," helped weigh the second draft.

"Not bad," said Dynamite. "Not bad for a city bred."

"Listen, small man, I was punching cows before you was born," replied Done Movin', and stuck Dynamite affectionately with a pencil. He was a grinning man, fat, with bad teeth and he wore brown whipcord trousers and khaki shirt and a chauffeur's cap on the back of his head with three Union buttons pinned to it.

Dynamite assailed him one more: "How'd you happen to git here first? Most times you piddle in 'long about the middle of next week." And they insulted each other back and forth while Dynamite weighed the cattle and I waited by the door, wondering what it might be to stand in front of 14,228 pounds of terror-stricken beef.

Dynamite gave his okay.

I had the sudden inspiration not to open the door very wide and then the cattle might pour out thinly like anything else. I cracked the door a few feet. A yearling nosed out suspiciously, another followed, and another was three and then ten thousand yearlings hit the door and the door hit me and I went down against the fence and stayed there while the side of my head took fire slowly and the stars went round and round.

Dynamite poked his face out. "Hey cowboy? All right?" Then he saw me and began to laugh. Done Movin' came and the moment he saw me his face brightened and he joined Dynamite in a truly hearty laugh. "Don't never stand *behind* a door thataway," said Dynamite. "You'll get killed. Open the thing wide and stand out front where they can see ye."

As I came back inside the scales, holding my head in a handkerchief, Done Movin' was reminded of a story: "Like the other day I had my racks off and went to hauling grain. So I had a flat right in front of that asylum there in Napa and got my tools out and went to work. D'rectly this guy come along, decent enough, 'bout fifty I'd say, could have been anybody's daddy, and he starts a-axing questions. Axed me what I done and I told him. Axed me how much I had on and I could tell him to a pound, 31,180 'cause I'd just weighed-in at the Bridge. 'Thirty-one thousand,' he says, just as polite, and 'Thank you,' and he walks away. Well, I changed my tire and drove along and was gettin' in towards Napa when I heard the siren. 'Say,' the copper tells me, 'you run over a guy back there.' He's kindy severe. 'Nossir,' I says, 'I never run over nobody; not that I know of.' 'You come along with me,' he says. So we turn around together and go back, nine mile, maybe ten, and we get to the asylum and right there in front is the feller who'd been axing me them questions. He's kind of down and out, fact is he's plastered to the pavement like a postage stamp. . . . A looney, see? He'd been trying to do it a long time, and when he did get loose he axed me all them questions so polite and then just walked around between the truck and trailer and laid down."

"Well, I'll be goddamned," said Dynamite.

"Yessir," said Done Movin', "that's what happened. Here," he said, "sign my ticket. I gotta be in Reno this time tomorrow." He held out a bill of lading and Dynamite signed it and kept the carbon duplicate. "Moller oughta be here any time. He was right behind me at the river, but the drawbridge got him."

"Good old Commodore," said Dynamite. "That'll make him ornerier 'n buckskin. He sure hates not to be first."

"Well, take it easy boys!" said Done Movin' and was on his way.

We stood outside the scales and watched the big Diesel pull away into the mist, heard it shift for the slope by the beet-pulp pit, and shift again for the level of the county road, and go away up into the hills till only an echo came back faintly, like the baying of a hound.

"One gone," said Dynamite. "One gone and a dozen to go. We may as well get back to sleep."

He spoke of Moller who would bring the next truck in. They called him "Commodore" because he told everybody what to do and they laughed at him because he had no authority. He'd kill himself to get in first; never stopped for a beer and a sandwich, only for fuel. And once in a while, when he telephoned home to get his orders as all drivers did, and the dispatcher gave him orders for the others, too, he had his reward.

We heard another Diesel roar and the sound of heavy gears working on the turn beyond the barn. The Commodore was coming.

This time Dynamite left me alone and went away to fix the gates in the alley and balance the scales. In the darkness, my head still burning, I watched the Commodore roll up slowly and put the door of his truck even with the chute on the first try—a pretty good piece of work for after midnight. The engine idled down, the Commodore got out and stopped before the headlights to look at his watch, and next moment he stood beside me on the dark strip of footboard that runs along a cattle chute, just the outline of him against the fog.

"Well, you made her," I said.

"Yeah," said the Commodore, sympathetic as stone. "Where's Dynamite?"

"Down the line."

"Anyone ahead of me?"

"One," I said.

"Who was it, Henry?"

"A guy named Done Movin'."

"Well, that's Henry, ain't it? . . . I seen him at the Bridge."

I was trying to get the door open but couldn't because the Commodore had done such a good job of pulling up to the chute he had wedged it. "Here," said the Commodore, "lemme show ya." He jumped down and wrenched and tore the door away and counted the cattle carefully as they came off, twenty-four head, somehow managing always to keep his back to me, as though maybe I had shown myself a member of some inferior race, unworthy of a clear front view.

Ten minutes later a first draft was on the scales, but still no Commodore appeared. "Okay!" yelled Dynamite, and I remembered my job was to count cattle without being killed. Dynamite had said stand out in front. Dynamite had laughed loudly and long. The misgiving went through me like a sudden pain that Dynamite and Jaydee Jones were one of a kind. "Okay, okay!" sang Dynamite, "what's holdin' up the dee-tail?"

I barely put a finger on the latch. The heavy door leapt open and swung back and somehow there I was alone, just I, squarely in the black mouth of the scales, from where there came a bawling and a seething and a splintering of redwood, as though all hell were in there ready to break loose. But it didn't. Not an animal offered to move. My blood was running better and I took a step backward. A thin stream of yearlings trickled by. I counted them easily. When the stream became too large,

I stepped forward, thinning it. If the yearlings ran too thin, I stepped backward and their flow increased. There was nothing to it.

"Twenty-four head!" I yelled.

"That's what I got," boomed the voice of the Commodore like a grenade exploding in the little shed; yet it was meant for me—a hard kind of compliment. The Commodore explained to Dynamite why he had come late: "So when I got back from Phoenix, I told 'em I wasn't ready to go—I'd been out a hundred hours then—but they said, 'Now listen here, T. S. Ordway wants these cattle; and whose name is wrote bigger around here, his or yours?' That's what the dispatcher said. So I gassed up and hit the road. I was the last one into Havermeyers, last one loaded out. I lent a hand to all the other guys; not one of 'em stayed to help me. But I know that Strawberry cut-off, see, where she hits the ridge this side of Nelson's Corner, so I took a left on 88 and saved two hours and came in flying clear to the River Bridge, leading *all* the way. And there I had to stop and fuel and while the hose was in the tank I seen Henry's Number 4 go by, but I'd have caught him even yet if the goddammed drawbridge hadn't stopped me." As he thought of what this bridge had done, the lines in the face of the Commodore grew deeper still, like iron bands cutting into wood. He asked no sympathy; he gave the facts. He was a Prussian and he punished himself and his machine of rubber, steel, and Diesel oil with concrete miles, as he would have punished all flesh and blood until it submitted, or became steel. "If anyone wants me," he said as he was leaving, "I'll be at the Princess Hotel in Sacramento."

The Diesel roared full-throated; the air brakes sighed; the Commodore became an echo fading in the night.

Now trucks came rapidly—two at a time, three, four—and their snoring in the line before the barn, their many-colored twinkling lights and shouts and horns made the yard look like an estuary filled with ships, or a great river anchorage with vessels waiting for the tide. In the darkness men became voices. I swore and kicked and sweated over the dank and stinking beds of trucks with comrades I never saw—Oklahoma Dutch, plain Swedish, Spanish, the lingo of Portugee Bill who owned a pool hall in Tulare and ran a bookie business on the side. These men lived quickly and were gone, yet I had known them better than if I'd seen them face to face all day.

A stubby Irishman named Kelly had a spell of trouble. His cattle would not unload. He tried them in Ulster, in South Orange, in Brooklyn, and the best of Frisco cussing, but they wouldn't move. "Goddamn," he said, breathless on the rafters that hold the open bed of a truck apart, "come out ye sons-of-bitches, it's Kelly talkin'." And they came.

So the hours were used up. At three o'clock the wind blew the fog away and let us see the stars men know who work by night—late stars, somehow brighter and better than the ones you see around ten o'clock when most people go to bed. They splattered through the sky from north to south, dusty and brown, like somebody had run there with a bucket and spilled them. They looked down and they knew who worked and who didn't and who owns the world when everything lies quiet. A truck had just pulled away. Dynamite and I stood still in the alley and the voice of the wind came rising through the boards and rails reminding us that man is very small and the earth by night is very long and lonely.

We had good luck when the last three loads came in together, even Blue with the broken shaft; but these drivers, nineteen hours on the road, would not go home. They stood around the headlights of the first big Moreland Diesel, bills of lading signed, nothing to hold them but their cigarettes and talk of what had happened in the day: "It was just where the Grapevine hits concrete and makes four lanes, takes off steep there beyond Bakersfield ten mile. So Kelly had her flying high and wide, comin' off in over-drive, you know, with me a-chasin'. Right there was where he blowed 'er. Sure thought he was gone. . . . Took her to the fourth lane and met a tanker coming up, so he took her back and she hit the ditch with her right three and dug a furry and a cloud of dust you could see by the moon. And his load got shiftin' and the frames picked up the sway and he cut a wiggle like a snake down U.S. 44. Oh, I tell you, watching him was misery. I sweat cold. I wished the bastard would spill and put me out of pain, but he never—the crazy Irishman. I'd have jumped or prayed or done something sensible, but not him—not Kelly. He rode her through and brought her out the end a-weavin' in that traffic like a maiden through the daisy-chain. . . . "

A deputy dispatcher had come along, red-haired, clean, and young American as football and corduroy trousers. He told the others where to go. "Potts," he said, "you beat it to Eureka; lay over there. Call in tomorrow, Fresno Operator 13, and she'll tell you where to go. Blue, you get that propeller-shaft to the warehouse and after breakfast—that's six o'clock for you, that ain't very long now—you take Henley's Number 9 and meet Joe Streets at Appleton, the junction there, and he'll give you his load for the city and you take 'em right on in. He has to be at Winnemuca this time Monday to haul sheep and he's been out three days. Charlie, I don't care what the hell you do. You might even go to bed somewheres, but make damn sure it's alone!"

Minute after minute they lingered, stretching this longest hardest day until somebody mentioned steak, and the idea grew and finally it was agreed they should meet at a certain diner at a certain red neon sign where Highway 18 cuts the Danvers Slough. So they got in and gunned their motors till the sleeping yards roared back the sound, and with a shout and a touch of the horn they were gone off homeward in the night. We stood alone and listened for them shifting on familiar slopes and turns, and heard them baying far along the valley till at last no sound came back.

The job was done.

Day came rapidly as I crossed the silent quadrangle of garages and heard Dynamite's old Packard labor home. I entered the washroom to clean myself and have a drink—the night's work had dried me out—and there at the sink was Jaydee Jones washing with a bar of bright red soap.

I put my lips under a faucet and took a drink.

Jaydee rubbed his face hard with his towel. "B'lieve I've took the pleurisy," he said, rubbing his chest and shoulder vigorously. "Got *such* a pain." And he made circles in the air with his shoulder and right arm. I knew there was nothing in the world the matter with Jaydee, that Jaydee knew this and knew I knew it. Once burned and twice wary, I washed my hands and said nothing.

"That old bunkhouse," went on Jaydee. "That damned old *thing!* Why there's a westerly gale across't my cot I'd be proud to see Columbus have."

I suggested a compress of hot towels.

"Reckon so?" said Jaydee. "Dunno about hot towels. Had a little cousin Sally to git a lung blistered by a hot towel her mammy give her. . . . Oh, I reckon I *could* heat one just a little. But I kind o' hate to, thinkin' about what it done to Sally Mae. Git yore cattle in?"

"Yeah," I said, "We got 'em. Took us all night but we finally got 'em."

"You stayed with her, eh?" said Jaydee, looking out at me for the first time from under his towel. "W-e-l-l, my old daddy used to tell me what I done by night was worth twice what I could do by day, providin' I weren't caught at it."

Jaydee's dark expression never changed, but he didn't bother to go on rubbing with the towel. I began to wash. When Jaydee saw I had no soap, he said, "Here y'are. Use mine," and flipped me the bright red bar.

Afterwards I went indoors and sat on the edge of my bed and began unlacing two shoes that suddenly felt made of lead, not leather. I didn't want to sleep. I wanted to go back outside and talk longer with Jaydee; but some cranes that had been roosting in the cypress trees flew away, making harsh cries, and I watched them go across the field, trailing each other through the early light.

I lay down then and fell asleep, knowing, without bothering to care just why, that the El Dorado Investment Company had room for me.

ARKY BILLY AND THE DUKE

UNCLE Arky Billy was the only man I ever knew who could use the word "God" regularly and make it sound all right. This was easy for him to do because for forty years God had been as much a part of his life as Arkansas corn fritters and ham gravy, He owned a place in the Boston Mountains, good black bottom land, where corn grew higher than the tallest man and filled each roasting ear with solid gold. On the hill was a patch of timber, black oak and hickory, that in good acorn years was the finest place in the world to fatten a young hog. Uncle Billy got his mail Saturdays at Bidville, eight miles down the road, and stayed over that night with his first cousin Ephraim Hewlitt so that he could attend the meeting of the Holiest Church. Sometimes his missus went with him and sometimes she didn't, but most often she did because, as Uncle Billy told me many times, "I shore love that little old gal of mine, shore do."

Their nine children had married and scattered through the West and settled finally in Los Angeles. Much persuasion had made the old parents rent their farm and come to California, but one week was enough for Uncle Billy. "They sure wanted me to stay, down there," he'd laugh, "sitting in the sunshine, growing old . . . " and he would laugh and laugh. "But not for me. I've worked too many years. I lighted out after that one week and found me something to do."

The something he had found was piling manure for the El Dorado Investment Company seven days a week with a team and Fresno scraper. Uncle Billy didn't mind the seven days nor the manure either, not even on hot windy days when it dried and blew in your eyes and stung your nostrils till it seemed you were breathing fire, and he didn't mind the lousy bunkhouse nor the three dollars a day nor the privy, so long as he could get to town Saturday nights for the meeting of the Holiest Church.

The thing he minded most was evil. . . .

I didn't know Uncle Billy well when it happened. A week before, one of the fellows in our bunkhouse room quit and he moved in and took the empty bed. Duke McGraw had the one next it. He was a tough young fellow always with a shadow of red beard on his face and a pervading moroseness about his mouth and eyes. He had spent a good deal of time in the city, part of it in the prize ring, and fancied himself as pretty handy with his fists. He was the leader of a small group of similarly morose young men, two others to be exact, who had come from the same background. After supper they would gather by the Duke's bed and talk about "babes" and "dames" and "dough" and games of snooker down at Lucky Dick's. The rest of us would roll over against the wall and try to sleep. But you can't get away from that kind of people. They're like weeds in a garden—either you root them out or they root you. They have a lot to say, four-letter words mostly, and I noticed more and more of the other men, especially the younger ones, would listen in the evening, sitting at the table in the center of the room, pretending to be getting warm at the old wood stove, or maybe reading a magazine, but listening just the same.

So things stood the evening I came into the washroom after work, a little late because we'd taken two cars of steers to the railroad to ship, and a little fussed and tired because I'd pinched my right thumb in one of those vicious sliding doors the Southern Pacific put on their cattle cars.

I was trying to get that thumb washed without wetting the sore place when Uncle Billy came in, still in his black breeches and faded gray shirt, fresh from bedding down his black Percheron team after a long day in the. pens.

He sat behind me on the bench that runs along the

front of the showers, quietly a minute, breathing slowly the way an old man does at evening.

The water ran down over my hand into the sink; the stove that heated the water sparked and roared a little, but I was too tired to turn round and start talking to Uncle Billy.

"Bobby boy," he said quietly after a minute, "Bobby boy, the Lord sure was a-blessin' me out there today."

I remembered once that morning we had passed with cattle somewhere down wind from the old man and heard his voice rising in holy song, faintly, far away, like an old, old fiddle scraping.

I turned around and smiled to show I understood and saw the religious fire in his blue eyes—a little wild, that fire, but no matter. The face made you forget. It was an old American face, something from a daguerreotype that should have had a frame of gold, something made of the older American substance that made Lincoln's face and Jackson's, Sam Houston's and Davy Crockett's. Its lines were like the rivers draining a continent.

Uncle Billy looked at me and said gently, "Bobby boy, how does youall believe, one God Almighty?"

I thought a second and I nodded.

"Good boy. . . . " He smiled and shook his great head of black hair several times, imparting somehow an immense quantity of friendship. "There ain't no other way, no sir, no other way. I found the Lord a long time ago. I'd fought agin him many years. I'd had hard days and good, but hard mostly. Then after I opened my heart and let Him in, seemed like hardness went out of my life and I become a happy man. Seemed like after that everything I turned my hand to prospered, and I had bread where they was stones before. I bought my place and raised nine kids and worked many a long year into my old age, happy and well, with them as I loves around me. What more does a man ask?"

"Not much, Uncle Billy," I said.

"Take them young fellers in our room," he continued, "poor young 'uns. They's been too long in the city livin' out of paper bags. And now all God's green earth and sky can't clean 'em. They's a dirty clear inside. . . ." This brought a flicker of grief into the old man's eyes, and for a moment he shut them and sat there against the bleached boards of the shower wall. "Take them on your one hand, the Duke and all of them, and take the older fellers on your other and you have the beginning and the end. Never a home but an old bunkhouse fit for dogs, never a good woman nor a good laugh. Jesus says to them as has he will give the world; but first you gotta get Him, Hisself, and till you do, you ain't got nothing."

As Uncle Billy said this, the supper bell rang and he started up and said, "Gracious, Lord, there's supper. And me still in dirty hands and shirt!"

We went together in the back door of the bunkhouse and through the bare board rooms into our own. Uncle

Billy always changed his shirt for supper. He insisted I go ahead to the cookhouse so that Mike, the cook, wouldn't be put out.

Our Sunday night supper was always the same—roast pork, canned peas, mashed potatoes. The food was perfectly good, yet the very fact of it's being always the same gave the men great cause to grumble. Somehow it represented all the repetition of the week's work; and then on the Sabbath, the day of rest on which we all worked just the same, to come and find the same pork and potatoes and peas was more than they could stand.

The Arkansawyers expressed themselves about it by fancying what T. S. Ordway ate for Sunday supper—frog's legs fried in melted gold, roast pheasant stuffed with d-y-a-monds; for stomach he had a mint modeled after the big U.S. one in Frisco, and so on and so forth. But the followers of Duke had been to Frisco and seen the U. S. mint, and they sat together, the two of them, with an empty seat between for the Duke, with their heads hunched forward and their arms thrust out like animals' paws on the table around thick white plates of food. A thin weathering of tan lay on their faces the way stucco lies on a cheap building. They looked dirty. On either side sat men from Arkansas, Missouri, and every western state—men who had grown up in dirt and even now did not wash any more often than these two, but who looked clean.

I had taken a seat at the end of the table, not because we had any particular places, but because the thirty of us filled the benches as we came. I helped myself from one of several platters of roast pork and called for spuds and for "Hush puppy," Mike's own gravy, that brought a blessed silence to many a troubled dish. We were being served by a new flunky, a quick, freckled little man who had been a professional waiter and slipped around the room with plates stacked up and down each arm, apparently for no reason at all but to keep in practice. I saw Mike through the open door watch him with a look of real pleasure. Mike had been a highly paid cook himself once, back in the gold dust days of San Francisco; and he liked to tell about them and to wear a tall chef's cap and carry himself with the dignity befitting a professional man. I watched him now, stirring a giant black kettle on the giant black stove, as if he were an artist mixing pigments for his greatest painting; and his eyes followed the flunky lovingly.

Down the table three places, Jaydee had come up against the pork. He and Arkansas Jody discussed it for a while across the table, comparing it to the hog and hominy they had known back home and even entering the subject of the various remarkable hogs they had cut in their time.

"Once," said Jody, "me and Silas Williams was out a-huntin' possum with three good dawgs, hum-dingers they was, 'cause Silas was chary 'bout his dawgs. By the light of the moon we seen 'em start this hawg down where the crick bent round a meadow. She was a sow and what I mean she was an ornery hawg—ornerier 'n wild horse radish. She rattled them big choppers and got away, but we catched her baby—a gilt half-grown, right in the huckleberries there. Do you know, that was the finest bit of hawg ever I ate."

"Best hog I ate," said Jaydee, "was one time in Abilene. . . . Give me by a Jew. . . . I was a little old kid on the bum and I asked this guy for a quarter. 'No,' he says, 'are you hungry?' 'Starved,' I says. 'Come on,' says he, and took me into a café and told me to order a dinner. So I orders hog. When it come finally, I ate and ate, but that man never touched food to his lips. 'What's the matter,' I asked him, 'ain't you hungry?' 'Sure,' he said, 'I'm hungry. When I was a kid like you I was hungry all the time. I can't eat pork, though. . . .' Now ain't that funny? That guy didn't believe in hog? Why is that?"

Jody didn't know; so they called on Roy down the table to tell them why it was, but he didn't know either.

"Well," Jaydee said, "I know I can't eat *this* one without I do something more to him than old Mike done," and he said this loud enough for Mike in the kitchen to hear and smile. He reached a brown bottle from one of the clumps of strange sauces that stood like islands up and down the table and never under any circumstances were touched. "Reckon this 'll do 'er," he said. "Knew a old nigger mammy back home took this on her haid whenever she had the itch."

Jaydee made us all laugh. When the boys from Arkansas talked, Sunday supper became a success.

Eagerly we watched Jaydee unscrew the cap of the brown bottle. As he was about to pour from it, Uncle Billy came in. He should have sat at the end of the table because, although we had no definite places, it was the thing to do; but as he passed the empty seat between the disciples of the Duke, I saw him hesitate, thinking for just a second, and sit down. He wasn't welcome. These two gentlemen had said no decent word since Christmas, and they said none now. Uncle Billy helped himself to what he could reach and asked for other platters, but before setting anything down, he offered it to the young men. It was plain his being there bothered them. I saw one's expression begin to change and curl faintly into an ugly smile. Just as though the place between were empty he began talking to his friend about last Saturday night.

"That babe young Mace had—did you see her? She was a honey."

"Yeah," said the other, and they exchanged a wink, "she *sure* was a honey. She had everything but the bureau drawer. I don't see why she goes on giving that stuff away; she oughta get wise and sell a little of it." They made a nasty laugh together. Uncle Billy continued eating his supper. So did we all, with the corner of one eye and with every ear wide open.

We didn't wait long.

"You talk like the preacher done to Sadie the Red,

said it was a preacher started her in business." They made another nasty laugh, chewing their food at the same time, glancing slyly around to see how they were doing, and from up and down the table came the ribald little echoes. "Good old Sadie! So the preacher tells her she'll be okay wid the Lord if she repents and he says, 'Come around tonight at nine and we'll go through it together.'"

Uncle Billy asked for the mashed potatoes. He might have been back home having Sunday supper with Ephraim Hewlitt.

One of the young men wiped his mouth with the back of his hand, turned to Uncle Billy, and said sweetly: "Uncle Bill, how was it you told us the other night in the washroom that Lord Jesus came to you?"

The clinking of the forks on plates, the sound of a glass being set down, the heavy chewing of the men receded to a certain distance and remained, and the rasp of old Mike's spoon stirring in the kettle joined them far away, like the sound of a strange instrument heard only when the music fades.

Uncle Arky Billy continued eating his mashed potatoes.

He wiped his mouth and set his fork against one side of the plate and his knife against the other and looked out the window where there was still a kind of daylight. "When the Lord found me," he said, "I was earning fifty cents a day and my dinner, a-snakin' black oak logs down Jenkin's Hill." The gloom was comfortable; it made all the room the same and all of us, except Arky Billy, whose face happened to be squarely in the window light. "Them was the hardwood days, big days of work and not much money. All through the blue mountains from early morning till the supper bell you could hear them axes ring. I was twenty-eight year old, my daddy dead, old Ma and me a-takin' on the family. But I had vinegar in me then same as you boys and two-bits of every half-dollar stayed with me, 'cause since I was big enough to carry a hoe I'd gone into the fields and done my share, and now I figured that tune was gettin' old, see? I wanted time to live and a little fun while I lasted, 'cause I was young.

"So I went to town.

"That winter little Sister Amy died. One day in March when young green was just a-featherin' the trees, I started down Jenkin's Hill with a wagon-load of logs, six mules, and a brake-log dragging. No blacksmith ever built a brake could hold them loads. We chained a tree behind. I'd made it fine to Cherry Bench and curled the rawhide over them mules and skinned down the Holler Mill Grade where it takes out steep above the branch. Right when I'd got up on the bluff I felt her go. . . . That load drave over them mules like the Lord Jehovah done the Philistines in the time of David. In the shapin' of a word they was gone over the cliff, and the wheelers in their place was dead afore they reached the edge, crushed, for that load snapped apart and the logs was spears a-dravin' down the mountain. I fell amongst 'em, for'rd, under the single-trees, but they passed me by. Hairs o' my head was barbered by them wheels but I was spared. . . . I never looked to see my mules, best team then skinning in the hills. I went to where that brake-log laid. The chain'd parted in the middle. I picked it up and stood a while holding the broken end like a man does a place he's been fresh hurt. And then I knowed I was a sinner spared by God's grace and I repented me."

Uncle Billy said no more. The room was dark. Old Mike had quit the stove and leaned against the kitchen door with the great spoon hanging from one hand.

"Well, it's gettin' awful dark," said Mike after a time, and lit the bulb that hung on a cord from the ceiling. The men began to eat.

Uncle Billy turned to the fellow beside him: "That was how Jesus come to me. Afterwards I prospered. All a feller needs is to worship one Almighty God and love his neighbor like hisself. Those is the two great laws."

At first there was no answer but the clinking of the forks on china and the feeding of the men. Somebody asked for gravy. The young man took his face out of his plate and made a quick look around and said hurriedly: "Like old Giddy McGurdy, went to church and heard you was supposed to love thy neighbor; went home and he says, 'I'll begin right away with *mine!*' . . . Got along fine till her husband found out about it."

The room filled up with laughter. Somebody said, " 'T wasn't Duke done that, was it?" and as one man we laughed again till the place echoed. I saw the Duke had come in and was standing near the door. Everybody saw him but Uncle Billy.

The Duke moved forward and stood behind the old man. Since this was Sunday he had been drinking and was very bright and shiny. Now the Duke was no inconsiderable man. He stood about five-eleven and must have weighed a hundred and eighty. His face was short and square, the fighting proportion, although I don't think Duke ever had been more than a good second-rater in the ring, and his nose was spread around off-center and his ears had a look of steak that's been well-pounded. He sported red hair, combed pompadour, and always on his face that shadow of red beard. He put on suddenly an absurd expression, like a ham-actor when he knows he has the stage, stiffened one thumb, and did a little dance and dumb-show behind the old man's back, ending with a foul gesture.

We snickered.

Duke stiffened both his thumbs and jabbed them into Uncle Billy's back the way a criminal would use two guns. "Old Arkansawyer, I b'lieve you're in the wrong seat!"

Uncle Billy's head was bent; the top of a fork stuck

out of his right fist. His face got huckleberry red, then white, then gray-pale the color of aspen bark. All at once he rose right up, fork in hand, and spun around and his eyes went over Duke like fire in the hills goes over brush. He took a step, and something of a smile came out on Duke; he began to sway and fade, moving from the hips, and automatically his hands went up and found their place. Uncle Billy's arm and fork were back, the arm that in the hardwood days had laid down oaks. His face was a covering of anger, dark red, stretched thinly on white bone.

The arm swung down; the Duke swayed backward from his hips, hands in place, uncoiling like a snake from danger and his smile grew bright and wide. But Uncle Billy's arm rose slowly and he said, showing the fork: "Does these belong to any man?"

The Duke drew back his lips and laughed. Uncle Billy picked up knife and fork and spoon, put them on his plate, and came slowly toward the end of the table, passing behind a row of silent heads, each in its plate.

Duke chuckled and sat down, but there was no mirth in him. He took hold of platters and slid food onto his plate but his eyes were for the men around, and his jaw cocked ready to snap, and every-so-often he ran a hand twice quickly through his red pompadour.

Uncle Billy was not eating; he stood up all at once and threw his fork onto his plate till the heavy china rang, and when he left the room the glasses on the table shook. Duke watched him every step, sidewise, like a proud dog. After the door had shut he laughed and said: "Gonna go and say a prayer, I guess!" and then looked around quickly to see if anyone gainsaid this. But none did. We bent our eyes upon our plates and laughed dutifully.

Supper over, we strolled under the cypress trees back toward the bunkhouse. Almost no wind blew—a rare thing that happened in this country only at evening and only at this time of year, early in October, when the long days shorten and for a while come silently and warm. Behind the bunkhouse, across the road, cattle were moving in the shadow, and dust from the pens rose round them slowly, as though the ground were burning. Beside us toward the sunset a stubble field descended many miles to salt marshes and the bay. Down there we saw a figure moving in the field, bent forward and alone.

Roy took my arm and pointed, "The old man's down there a-havin' it out, him and the Almighty."

In our bunkhouse room two bulbs were lit and the Duke talked and lay upon his bed with his followers around him, some on the floor, some seated on boxes, listening. He told about a three-year hitch he'd done in the Army at Honolulu: "Easy? You can't beat the Army for a soft time. Two o'clock and you're done for the day. All you gotta do is be athletic. We held the baseball championship three years; I pitched a little myself though fighting was my main line."

The alcohol had left the Duke, his smile had gone,

and his eyes got shifty, finding the door often. He showed a diamond on the fourth finger of his left hand. "Frisco," he said. "Frisco's got plenty of these if a feller knows where to find 'em. Jesus, I wonder why I stick around this place. There's no dough where cattle's being made. Year I fought Spider Fallon—'31 it was, no, '32; I never fought the Spider till '32—I ate nothing all that year but New York cuts. No sir; 365 days! But that's the way I am: if I take a notion to something, I don't care how small it is or how unimportant, Duke's gotta have it or his name ain't Duke. Like that old man tonight—son-of-a-bitch, I didn't give a damn about him. He's no skin off my tail. It's just the idea, that's all. Why, hell . . ."

Outside somebody was coming on the boardwalk, the one Jim Magee laid early that year to keep our feet dry. Duke's talk began to wobble. His words ran out of places to go. They went up and down and got jiggly, like a man walking with one leg shorter than the other. "Why, hell, Jesus, and for Christ's sake!" The steps came on, heavy, hollow, on their way.

Duke sat upon the edge of his bed and wiped a hand over his mouth and chin.

Uncle Arky Billy came in the door. He looked like a man who has been very ill. He stood and let the screen spring gently shut behind, against his hand, and it seemed this took five minutes.

"Duke," said Uncle Billy and never moved. "Duke,"

he said, "I've delivered my soul; I'm free from your blood."

Duke didn't do a thing, didn't look as though he'd care to, except he took hold of the bed with one hand.

Uncle Billy crossed the room and began taking off his shirt by the bed in the corner. This action spread his very white body under the light, weathered at the wrists and neck by sun and wind; and we saw low mounds of biceps, mountains that had washed away, and traced the lines of lifting muscles like a harness up the back. All were there, still working, still good. Uncle Billy had a lot of flesh to handle.

Somebody touched the string of the electric light and the shadow ran in arcs and circles on the old man's body. He took off black pants and shoes and drew a blanket over him as he lay down.

During all this time the rest of us had stood and stared, following everything he did, and made no sound. Now one of the boys said: "Well, how about a game of Pedro?"

He got two answers and, after urging some time for another, persuaded the young fellow who had talked to Uncle Billy at supper—Sugar was the only name I ever knew him by. He stood up sheepishly from a box beside the Duke and went over to the table.

After a couple of hands an argument developed over the best method of play, Sugar saying Ellan Butts was crazy for not having led the ace. "Aw, you're nuts!"

said Ellan. "That way, unless you got the Pedro, we lose him sure."

The argument went along so well that even the second young man—"Mac," we called him—who had been sitting on the floor with his back against the Duke's bed, came over to listen, so that Duke was left alone fingering his diamond.

The disagreement got nowhere except up, just like a fire, and finally Sugar turned in his chair and called out: "Say, Uncle Bill—ain't it good Pedro to lead the ace on the first round?"

The old man lay still, speaking to the bare boards of the ceiling.

"Sure thing it is, Sugar boy. That way you stand to take the Pedro more often than you lose him; and a man can't 'spect to take hisself a trick every time, you know."

Sugar put up a cheer for himself. "See there, dummy," he said across the table, "whad'd I tell ya?"

THE HAPPY MAN

As soon as Blackwell's man came into the Last Saloon we saw he was on his Christmas party. That was his trouble—trying to be happy once a year. His face wore hair and he wore three shirts (which meant he'd been out six days), two hickory-grays and a Frisco dandy at the bottom that should have had a collar but had only a gold button in the middle of the throat. He was the stingiest man in the world, that man of Blackwell's. Why, he was so stingy he wouldn't buy the soap to do his laundry, but waited until Mrs. Blackwell did hers and then used the dirty water. All year long he never spent a dime, but at Christmas he would take a week off and go to Frisco and tie one on. He always rode back home in a taxi—we could hear it outside, purring for him to come, telling you he had plenty of money but not much time. Said he'd seen rich city folk ride past all year and hang their face at him and he wanted to see how it was done. Sometimes he would keep the cab a week, riding around, looking at things, and when he took the notion, he would have it stopped so he could sleep, and when a shirt got over-ripe he would go to Abel's General Store and buy another. That was why three shirts meant he had been out a week.

But Blackwell's man didn't look happy. He passed right by us at the table and headed for the bar where Pete, our saloonkeeper, was leaning on his hand, under a blue eyeshade, thinking about Christmas.

"Howdy, Santa Claus," said Blackwell's man, "what's old Santa got for good boys that is thirsty?"

"Tom and Cherry," said Pete. "Specials." Pete was a Dane and he sort of chewed his words, and his gray mustache in between times.

"Who?" said Blackwell's man.

Behind the bar was a mirror that reflected the suspenders crossing on Pete's back and his apron strings and the backs of all the bottles set on shelves along the mirror. Even more conspicuously it reflected a great big bowl of something hot that gave off steam enough to wet the glass and made a heavenly image, all of gold, that tilted up a little, as though this stuff were just too wonderful to stay on earth.

Pete indicated it to Blackwell's man with the smallest motion of one hand, and Blackwell's man looked very happy all of a sudden and said, "Gimme some, Pete."

Pete filled a coffee mug and set it steaming on the bar. They muttered over it a while and we sat and tried to hear them and the wind talked around the corners of the Last Saloon and didn't sound like Christmas Eve at all.

"Pete," said Blackwell's man, "it's too sweet. Gimme something to cut it, something sour."

Pete mixed him up a whisky sour; but when he drank it, the lemon mingled with the sweetness of the Tom and Jerry and came out in between, like castor oil.

"Jesus!" said Blackwell's man, not looking very happy. "Why don't you learn to mix drinks, Pete? Or get some bottles ready-mixed like Frisco has?"

He tried a shot of straight Bourbon and then began arguing with Pete and finally blew clear up and went away just as happy as he had come.

He let in wind that made us shrink and shiver right on through to our gizzards. That wind was a cross between rheumatism and a fog. It blew all the time, straight from salt marshes and the bay; and on Christmas Eve it followed Dynamite and Cherokee and me clear to the doorstep of the Last Saloon, and blew us indoors with a whoosh and a stomp and said, "Now celebrate your Christmas!"

I don't know what there was to celebrate. We had to be at work by six the next morning. We worked on Christmas Day and Sunday because cattle are just as hungry then as on any other day. One of Dynamite's boys was down with the measles. Cherokee's wife was back in Oklahoma with her family. I was a young kid a long way from home. But you know how fellows get after a while—they just have to celebrate something even if they make it up.

So there we were, and we called for Pete to fill us up again with Tom and Jerry.

He came along, saying about Blackwell's man, "Poor fool. . . . Didn't have no coat, didn't have no hat. When he tries to buy a bottle, I tell him, 'No, you've had enough.' He never will be happy."

"No," said Cherokee, "not if he lives a hundred years and goes to Frisco every day."

"No," said Pete, "he'll never be happy."

"Not like we are anyway," said Dynamite. "Nobody could be happy quite like we are," and he made his blue eyes spark and his small young body shake and wiggle and become alive all over. He said, "I knowed a feller once was happy."

"Plumb happy?" said Cherokee.

"Plumb happy," said Dynamite.

"Didn't have no Sunday job?" I said.

"Nope."

"Didn't have no wife or kids?" said Pete.

"Nope."

"Well, let's hear about him," Cherokee said.

"Okay," said Dynamite. "It starts back home in Utah years ago. . . . Feller gets off a train, important feller too, 'cause this was the Continental Comet, see, and she used to smoke through Red Jewel like a streak of light. But she stopped for him; and the railroaders gathered and yessed him up and down and cost him plenty before they was through and he could stand alone and let me see him. Now he was the unlikeliest feller you *ever* saw—small, pale, kind of humpy, but he had a maverick's look in his eye and the air got away behind him when *he* moved.

"D'rectly the train took off and whipped him with its tail of dust and he stands there, a bag in each hand, faced south across the desert towards the mountains, and never knows she's gone. Then he sees me standing there and quits his bags and comes and says to me, 'I want to go down there.' And do you know all he done was point a hand down south?

" 'Sure,' I says.

" 'Fine,' says he, 'when do we start?'

" 'In the morning,' I says, 'I'll get the ponies.'

"So I puts him up at the Princess Hotel, M. M. Berg proprietor, and gets a hippy sorrel horse from Hap, my pard, and about then I remember all this guy has said to me, or me to him, has been yes, no—bang-bang.

"Next morning bright and early I and the ponies was at the Hotel and out he steps in a brand new pair of jeans and denim jumper that I knowed he'd bought from Charlie Pell across the street 'cause I could tell Charlie's denim when I seen it.

" 'Ready to go?' I says.

" 'Ready to go!' says he.

"With that he climbs aboard; and when I seen him do it, I could tell he'd rode a horse maybe once, maybe twice.

" 'You're traveling kind of light,' I says.

" 'Yes,' he says, 'I am.'

" 'How far did you figure to go?'

" 'How far?' he says. 'Far as you like.' And he waves another hand down south—down where the mountains rose up big and blue. My spine begun to creep. There was stuff about this here guy I'd never seen before. Now he weren't a scientific kind, had no hammer for to bust up rocks and look inside, no nets nor bottles nor even a pencil—just his clothes and a silly kind of straw hat Charlie Pell had sold him. I couldn't figure it.

"I says to him, 'We can ride till Christmas and it won't bother me. I know folks as will put us up at night for a good long ways at least.'

" 'Fine,' he says.

"So we took off. We rode all day across the desert, heading for the mountains that stayed always just as blue and far away, and when I seen him ride I knowed there was no question of this feller having ridden once or twice before, it was only once. The sour alkali got in his nose and made him sneeze. The new blue denim chafed his legs till they was rare as minute steak—I knowed; I could tell it in the way he set his horse, cocked forward like a little boy that's whipped and can't sit down. He never said a word. I couldn't tell if he were sad or happy or just thinking hard. We rode and rode and the sun got up and hit that desert square and bounced right back like fire from a red-hot stove. This feller's face swole up till he couldn't see the mountains he was riding for; his eyes run; and when I asked him how he felt, he made a speech and says to me: 'Fine.'

"Well, I was a little whipped myself when, just at dark, we rode into Hoopaloo's place on Tank Crick out of Skull Valley. 'How far are we from the mountains now?' he says. 'We'll be there this time tomorrow,' I says, and hearing it he wants to look cheerful but can't because his face is burnt so it has no play left in it. He gets off kindy sudden—like a bag of flour that's had its bottom cut, and grabs the horn to keep from falling. I says to myself, 'You little son-of-a-bitch, you're game whatever you are.'

"For two days he couldn't travel and we laid up there with Hoopaloo, eating jerky stew and beans, but what he ate made him sick and we laid him over one day more. His face stayed raw as fire. We doctored it with bacon grease—with a rag on the end of a stick. It was Hoop's idea, not mine. He said it was the boss stuff for burns, though a shade salty. I bet the little gentleman could have said a good deal more about it, but he didn't. All he said was 'Thank-you-very-much-indeed!' bright and sudden like a lark, and it always made Hoop jump a little.

"Come the fourth day and we rolled out early, Hoop

and I, to do the chores, and he rolls with us. 'That's all right,' we tell him, 'there's nothing much to do.'

"'No,' he says, 'I want to help. I'll feed the chickens.'

"Later I meets him leaving the chickenyard. His face is kind of seared over now, half-brown, half-red, like a piece of meat on a quick fire.

"'Did I give them enough?' he says.

"'Yes,' I says, 'you did.'

"The yard was only ankle-deep in wheat.

"'I'm very fond of chickens,' he says. . . . Damn his soul! You couldn't help but like him.

"Then we hit the trail and by noon was in a country of scrub cedar—little old trees ten foot high that tried to be a forest and never made it but was built just proper for their size. The little gentleman said they was like the people of the earth that was cut small out of a big pattern.

"By noon we traveled in a country that was tall and green, where water run cold out of the stone. There was meadows—spots of shining sun where a man would want to stop and spend his life. There were ferns and flowers and the smack of trout hitting the water after flies, everything a man could ask, but it wasn't good enough for him. 'What's on the other side?' he says.

"By four o'clock the trees was growing thinner and the rocks whiter and I knowed the timberline was due. That would fetch him round, I figured. He could see from there till his eyes ached.

"We come upon a pass in a country where the trees

is old before they're born and the granite lays in rocks and slabs and the rivers is no bigger than your arm. 'Over this pass,' he says, 'what is there?'

"We ride along in shadow, cold, echoing ourselves from rock and snow, and come out finally on a slope where we can see and the sun lays still. There below us is the Twilight Country, the widest country in the world. Far to the south she goes, gray and rolling as the ocean on a cloudy day; and in her canyons are the shadows of gray heat that lie till evening. She's bare and empty as the sea and far around her rim she seems to burn, which is the heat-smoke rising. She's like a dish stuck in a fire, heaped with all the mountains of the world.

"'That's where I want to go,' says the little gentleman.

"'You can't,' I says.

"'Why not?' says he.

"'There ain't nobody goes to the Twilight Country,' I says.

"I told him of the water and the acid in the rocks, of winds that open on you like an oven door, of chambers in the stone that lets up gasses from the underworld.

"'Of course,' he says, 'of course. I ought to go alone.'

"We turned around then and started home.

"Away that autumn word come to me in Red Jewel how a feller crossing by the Twilight Hills had found a mule, runaway mule, and d'rectly he come along himself leading that mule, and Eben James who owns the livery stable said it was his mule—one he'd sold my little gentleman. Then the cry got up and come around to me as being last to see the man. 'Sure,' I says, 'I know where he is; I'll find him.'

"So I gets Hap, my pard, who can track a bird through the air, and with him four good horses, grub, bedding, canvas bags for water, and we travels and finds the place this feller says he caught the mule. It's up again a rim rock in a canyon that was long and gray and quiet as the grave. We made our camp and all night long the falling stones kept us awake—just pebbles, that's all they was, but they made you creepy thinking the ground alive.

" 'Fore ever day reddened in the east, we was clopping on the trail. South, we went, and south, going up that canyon while the trail roughened out and quit and the walls rose higher till they kept our sound for minutes before they gave it back. We never heard a living noise nor seen a sign till Hap stood by a flat stone and showed me where the mule had scuffed his shoe there coming down. A hind shoe, he said. To me it looked like maybe somebody struck a match there ten years ago.

"We worked all day to find that canyon's head; we clumb by running water that was cold and sweet, through boulders that was big as buildings and no trees. We come upon a place and I sees the water running backwards and looks and stares and says to Hap, 'See that water?' And that water run *down* hill!

"Ever come along a road and see a stile built over a fence? You say: 'Gee-whiz, Farmer Brown's built him a stile. Wonder why? Must be for something special or he wouldn't have taken all the trouble.' Well, that's how we felt that minute in that headless canyon, like some big Farmer Brown had been a-doing special things with the face of the earth, and left a place for us to wander up and over, to climb on down and see.

"And what we seen!

"She fanned down gradual a hundred miles, brown and bare and stony, and far down there what looked like rocks, and made an eddy in her like a stone in water, was really mountains. Gray walls begun on either side and reached up white to snow, and dirt flowed out of 'em like water. It half-way filled the canyons and, higher still, them walls was colored red, yellow, orange, in a stain that rose and quit right sudden, like some time years ago a great big colored sea had filled the valley just so high. Above was gray, except where slides had gashed her white, and I figured, after studying a spell, that was because the heat-smoke in the summer rose and stayed right at that line of colors and made them twi-lights through the canyons and shut the sun off like a big umbrella, while all above was cooked plumb out to gray.

"Even now in winter the ground laid under shadow and the sun come pale and you kept looking up and looking up, thinking it was gonna rain but it weren't.

That was the shadow in the air and it set your skin to creep.

"Dirt and stone was dumped in loose and helter-skelter like people dumps in piles in city lots when they're about to build, only these here piles was mountain chains. There weren't no trees nor brush nor other stuff that didn't matter or could go on later. This here was raw stuff from the beginning and boy, believe me, you could have built the world again with what we seen —and had a lot to spare!

"She was too big to mention so we never tried.

"Hap says to me, 'Our mule passed here.' He points me out a hole where water had been once and then mud and now a kind of whitish-yellow stuff that was like concrete only harder, and it stunk. There was rings of green and yellow round the edge that was the stain of acid from the rocks, and two little holes right in the center that looked like someone'd walked out there on stilts, and they was the marks of the forelegs of our mule. 'He tried to drink here,' Hap says.

" 'He must have been a thirsty mule,' says I.

"So we kept along and the canyons multiplied and run together and had no end and no beginning nor any meaning that was good that we could see, and Hap followed where that mule had gone like the flying birds follows the spring. We come on sudden valleys where the grass was green and water blue and always still, and all the sounds were echoes. We rode past bridges built by wind and water out of stone where God lives in the rock, as the Indians say, and casts the only rightful shadow in that land; and when we seen His shadow lying on our trail we chilled, picked up, and hurried through.

"At night we heard a noise like somewheres far away a furnace door was open, and next morning, if we passed that place, we'd find the little birds all dead beside the trail and see the palest shadow going on the hills for miles, and that was where the wind had cut the stone.

"There was no sound by night or day we'd ever heard or liked, till one morning in the early darkness I heard a rooster crow. 'Hap,' I says, 'wake up!'

"It come again.

"'Jesus,' he says, 'a rooster!' and buries his head.

"I says, 'Don't be a fool. Our little gentleman was fond of chickens.'

"Right over a hummock in a valley that was green as spring, by water as made all the noises of the sea, we found his camp. New grass was coming on it. The willows of the table had begun to sprout. His bed was puffed up mealy by the rain; and on a cedar stump this rooster set and give the sun hello. All around him, henfolk scratched and bustled after early worms and never heard a word.

"Hap says, ''Pears like he ain't gathered many eggs of late, that little gentleman.'

"And Hap was right. He looked and looked but this here trail was one he couldn't follow and some place, though I couldn't say right where, it led up in the sky, I knowed.

"Then we traveled and went out the way we'd came, and as we passed them rocks and steeps we had a feeling like the shutting of a thousand doors; and when we got to Red Jewel, the people that had been so hot for us to start had plumb forgot we'd gone. As for the little gentleman's folks, they never showed, they never gave a damn, they was no good; and the Continental Comet, she run through Red Jewel like a tongue of flame, as she does still, and never stopped again. . . . No, sir," said Dynamite—which meant his story was over—"she never stopped again."

We came back to the Last Saloon altogether in one breath, our eyes meeting as we drew it in and our feet scraping the floor, remembering how cramped they were and tired.

"He left nothing?" Pete said.

"Nothing," said Dynamite.

"What made you think he was so happy?" said Cherokee. "Why?"

"Why?" said Dynamite. "Well, I don't know. . . . I used to wonder why myself. He never was a happy man to see. And then I figured it was this: he'd pitched his camp in the country he liked best and never had to break it up."

We thought on that some time while the wind pecked and whined around the corners of the Last Saloon.

"Maybe so," said Cherokee, "but me, I'd settle for a lot less than he done. If I could lay a-bed on Christmas morning, I think I'd settle for that."

Pete said, "Same with me, too."

"Well, fellers," said Cherokee, stretching himself, "six o'clock will be here soon; we'd better move."

We said so-long to Pete and went outside and drove away in Cherokee's 1924 Dodge touring, with the wind hammering the isinglass and the faintest kind of shadow coming on the fields that would soon be Christmas.

THE SILVER BULLET

THIS is the story of Happy Jack Patee, who lived fast and died easy. He was just a guy, the cheerfullest I ever knew. He left Missouri when he was fourteen with a string of reefers on the Santa Fe line. He came like a rocket on the Fourth of July, up into the blue night of summer, and was all over in a minute. But he'll live forever because we'd seen him.

He can tell his own story. Jack talked better than most people his size and weight. Other guys will talk, too, but they are like the ones that spar with the champ—a round or two and they're done.

First, the time: noon of the rainy Christmas, 1940. The place: our garage and machine shop. By noon the rain had stopped, and a tule fog come down, the floating rheumatism of the Sacramento Valley, California, so thick you couldn't see your best friend six feet away. It goes straight to your bones no matter what you wear outside. We were sitting close around the stove that Al, Co. mechanic, had made from an empty oil drum. Our lunch pails lay open on a strip of concrete that ran between the bumpers of two V-8 trucks and a dirty work-bench where Al had spread some pinion gears and a hundred thousand greasy tools.

Beyond the windows white air was blowing, dead and cold.

Happy Jack sat close beside the stove. He had come in with the crew from the giant hammer mill that smashes hay for the cattle. He is fat and sassy, sitting on a block of wood, one arm akimbo, the other propping up a sandwich—what used to be a sandwich. His face is round and cherry-red from coming suddenly indoors; a purple scar from his mouth out along his jaw almost to his right ear makes his smile the wider. Altogether, he looks like a happy boiler with side-pipes leading in.

"*Rum,*" says Jack, and from the way he says it you know that rum will lose this round. "First rum ever I had was give me one time by a Shriner in Kansas City. I didn't care; he give it, so I took it. And you know, that was the only time *ever* I had a bottle of something I couldn't drink. One swaller and I run in a circle ten minutes."

"Likely you was hoggish," said Sims, who was opposed to Jack on the question of rum. "Rum is a gentleman's drink and has got to be accumulated easy, not all at one swaller. Besides, it was rum in general we was considering, not just one drink."

"Yeah," said Jack innocently, "yeah," so that you knew a murder was coming. "Like I used to be every time I'd kiss my wife, considering not her only but all the world o' women."

Sims shut up and ate his dinner like a gentleman.

Little Jody came in late. Born twenty years ago in Arkansas, he had grown up too thin, too scary, with weak eyes. You just couldn't help picking on Jody. "I'm cold," he said. "Honest to God, I am," and he crowded the stove.

"Quit sending money to yore Arkansas woman," said Cherokee, "and buy some clothes."

"Not clothes," said Jack. "Buy whisky; it's warmer by a dang sight."

"No, sir," said Jody. "Tried that all one winter and it never worked. Spring I come out wearing just my smile; it weren't enough." His back was against the stove, toward Happy Jack, with a pocket gaping open as denim pockets will. Jack slipped his cigarette inside, and all of us but Jody saw him.

"I never buy no clothes," said Happy Jack. "I got 'em staked around all over the United States—Michigan, Missouri, Illinois. I got one thirty-two dollar and a half suit as far east as Aspen, Indiana. . . . Good old Aspen. Had to kick the dew out of a feller there once't."

"Just had to do it, eh?" said Jody, innocent of evil

as a newborn child, a curl of smoke climbing his back. We died to keep our faces straight.

"Yeah," said Jack, "he was a-askin' me several times."

"Fought back, did he?" said Jody.

"Yeah, the son-of-a-bitch," said Jack, "he had no manners." Happy Jack dug a silver bullet out of his pocket and bounced it on one hand. "Tried to swipe my silver bullet . . ."

Jody went up in the air, clawing at his bottom like a cat that has been well turpentined. Words don't tell the sound he made; and you never knew the meaning of undress if you didn't see Jody on that Christmas day, peeling down his breeches and his drawers.

"Jody, put on your clothes!" said Jack, "This here's no time for *ro*-mance."

"Romance, hell," said Jody, trying to look over both shoulders at once, "this here's arson."

"Put on your clothes," said Jack, bouncing his silver bullet. "I want to tell these boys a story about the guy in Aspen, Indiana, who tried to swipe my silver bullet, my pretty silver bullet, the lucky Spanish bullet my old daddy give me."

"God damn you," said Jody, high up, like a little girl, "I'll get you!" but he took his laughing—a good guy, that Jody.

"I was number seven," continued Jack, "last of the boys. Says old Dad: 'Lucky seven, lucky silver.' (Dad was speakin' minus a leg at the time.) 'You came last and you'll go farthest. This here's yours, don't never lose it. Remember, everything just happens and don't you be there with your hands in your pockets, unless it's cold. Keep moving. A bullet's got the right idea. . . .' See, that's how he come to be minus a leg, stopping on the battlefield to pick up this here bullet. Poor old Dad, dead now. D'rectly after giving me this gift he went out one morning by hisself, into the shed, and undertook to start the tractor while she stood in gear. We heard him first, found him mashed like a bug agin the back of the shed."

Happy Jack stopped playing with his silver bullet and his face grew sober—the only time I ever saw it so. "About this time," he said, "my oldest brother, Arthur, come home horizontal out of Oklahoma where he'd stopped a two-by-twelve from falling down a derrick. We rallied round, the rest of us, and made a settlement: if he'd stay home and tend to Ma he'd have the place as he does today. Then one by one the rest of us took out.

"I went up into Illinois and worked in the steel mills a while, quit and worked the brickyards of Aspen, Indiana, quit there and rode the rods east for Toledo. I was just turned fifteen at the time, when a feller knows more than all the rest of his life. So we got near Toledo and the boys starts a departure and I says, 'What's the matter?' and they says: 'Humpy Davis.' 'Well,' I says, 'it's a shame to walk when you can ride.'

"I rode on in and Humpy got me."

"Humpy Davis," said Cherokee. "The toughest railroad dick! But he worked the Denver yards, I seen him there in '36."

"That was later," said Jack, "after he'd built a rep-'tation. When I met him, he was still a-learnin', although for a beginner he done pretty good. He give me such a pistol whipping as I wouldn't care to remember. Broke my jaw, the son-of-a-bitch. I never could run on cinders.

"So I went up town spittin' a few teeth, lookin' for sympathy. When I seen the red light, I knowed I'd found it. They'll always help a feller, every time. A nice little middle-sized whore led me out back to the sink, washed me, got me bandaged and fed with cold mashed potatoes and whisky that was the best ever I tasted. They all come down to have a look at me—kimonos, trailing cigarettes. Oh, they got a big kick outta me. 'Kid,' they said, 'you're standing where no man has stood before. You don't know how lucky you are. You're in a pretty sacred place, kid.' They told me I'd have a scar the rest of my life and I said that didn't matter, it'd make my smile just that much bigger. They got a big kick outta that. 'Kid,' they said, 'you'd better come back and see us when you're growed up.'

"They told me where to go for easy money, one of them ritzy night spots. I waited till a guy come out in soup-and-fish totin' his dame. I put it on him and he commence't to dig as that kind always does when they got a dame along. He come up with four bits. 'Oh, Harold,' says the lady, 'look at the poor child.' He dug again and this time done better. I heard it crackle and knowed it would be good. 'Here,' he says, handing me a five, 'take care of yourself.'

"With that five-spot I got clear back to Illinois.

"Ten days before Christmas I landed in Chicago broke, with the wind coming off the lake as if a icebox door was open and all jobs filled. I'm tellin' you fellers, them days was *tough*. For a week at a time I never took these hands outside my pockets, and I could feel this silver bullet like a icicle agin my leg.

"One morning on the Avenue I felt it and begun to think, remembering what Dad'd said. 'What's the matter here?' I says. 'What's wrong? Movin' the feet and not the bean?' Right then I looked up and there was the Palace Hotel. I says: 'This here's no coincidence.' Then I begun to *use* the old bean as a man does when his stomach's empty.

"Directly the golden doors did swing and heads bow low and out comes a fine lady overlaid so deep in furs you couldn't tell it was a lady only by her feet and her intention—I reckon nothin' but a woman would have undertook the Avenue on such a day, and just for pleasure as she done. But woman's woman.

"I trailed along.

"She was easy, too awful easy. Said she had a boy herself somewhere's over the sea and if he'd just be home for Christmas she'd be the happiest lady in all the world. 'My child,' she says, 'where is your home?' 'Alberkerky,' I says, and to this day I don't know why. I tried to tag the state on, too, but couldn't remember what it was, so I just says, 'Alberkerky' and lets it stand, kind of choking off at the end where the state should have come in. 'Oh, my,' she says. 'Poor child.'

"With the money she give me I could have rode with the bankers to New York and bunked at the Ritz, but I figured it was only fair, being as she'd been so kind, for me to go to Alberkerky.

"So I went. But I never got there. Took the Union Pacific when I thought I had the Santa Fe and before I knowed it I had Omaha—*Omaha*, there's a town! You don't never need to go there. Just say it over a couple of times to yourself: Omaha, O-ma-ha!

"I stayed long enough for a rib steak and hooked a rattler west. . . . That was some ride; that was the time when Santy Claus become Rodriguez, Christmas day of '32, when we rode the gol-dinginest, singinest freight that ever rolled down Sherman Hill to old Cheyenne.

"There was me and Lemmy Sykes of Batten Rouge and a short heavy-set feller we called Hank.

"We had a Rocky Mountain Pullman first class, two doors both slidin', and bring your own heat. Cold? Oh, Anna-belle! Christmas day come over the ranges clear and blue. Off south there was a gray sun, somewheres down toward Alberkerky, too far for us to feel. But we hung our feet outdoors and done our best 'cause even the wind was warmer than inside. Christmas! . . . And we hadn't eat for a day and a half! A hundred miles back we'd run out of lies and so just set.

" 'Section camp,' says Lemmy, and wants us to close up and duck, but I says, 'No, let the doors stay open. They'd maybe freeze and us come off at Frisco stiff as lettuce.'

"What I mean it was cold weather.

"So we stayed open and got our Christmas.

"That section camp was nothing to be scairt about; we slowed a little and was by, and d'rectly there come a gentle scraping from above, ever so light, as a turtle might make crossin' a flat stone, but I heard it—ever since Humpy Davis I'd paid better attention. Right easy-like I gives a yawn and glances up and there's Rodriguez, just the face of him, hanging from the cross-beam of the door like a happy monkey upside down.

" '*Amigos*,' he says—you know how Mexicanos talk—and it like to have put Hank and Lemmy off into the Platte River, or whatever river it was.

" 'Easy, boys,' I says. 'Just a Mexican,' and to Rodriguez, hearty-like, 'cause after all it's Christmas: 'Come on down and have some turkey and plum puddin'.'

" 'Ah,' he says, and again, and got so pleased I thought he'd bust. Just how he'd come we couldn't see. The train was making fences out of telephone poles just at that time, and while we was a-wonderin', there he stood, half a jug of wine in one hand, all one long grin. Talk about your monkeys!

" 'Rodriguez!' he says, and we shakes hands all around, dropping our eyes modestly to keep 'em on that jug of wine. He bows and chuckles and takes a short tour around the car to get the lay o' things, see where the gentleman's room was, the bar, the magazines, and best spittoons; and then he comes back and holds up the jug and I'm telling you he was like one of them little beans that jumps in Mexico—he just couldn't stay on the ground.

" 'Drink,' he says. 'Christmas, Christmas!' and we didn't keep him waiting. He wanted to tell us something: 'Birtay,' 'Birday,' it sounded like and when I said it for him, *Birthday*, he really did go mad. 'Yes, yes!' he says. '*Nacimiento*! Me!' he says, stabbing himself with a finger, and then upwards. 'Him, too.' And Hank, the God damned dummy, he looks up at the roof of the car and looks and looks but don't see nothin'.

"Well, we had a little party. Rodriguez turned out quite a talker, but what he give us come in pieces: He was working for the railroad up the line and got a week off after I don't know how many years; worked for three dollars a day, but he had lots of friends. Cheyenne was his next stop. He knowed a gal there named Rosita, real classy, lived in a little house on Elm Street with her sister Maria, roses in the front garden, you know, as the Spanish like, but no paint on the house. They expected him once a year; this was his birthday, his party. Well, he carried on. Said he didn't have to ride with us except he liked to, could have rid the caboose. He knew the boys, all *amigos*—anyway, by that time all the world was *amigos*, the jug of wine being shrunk considerable.

"Furthermore, he says he didn't ride cabooses 'cause they was too slow, hot, and stuffy. He'd worked a hand car all his life, outdoors, wanted open air, and the sweetest treat on earth for him was to ride the big trains he'd gotten off the track for all his life; and if accidentally we was to meet Manuel and Pasquale, and a guy named Romero and run them off the track, then Rodriguez was a-gonna be a-walkin' in the sky, plumb tickled.

"So there he was like a kid on a merry-go-round.

"D'rectly though, the wine give out.

"Then up a little grade ahead we seen a water tank by a lone tree and a string of house-cars on a siding. 'Oy-oy!' says Rodriguez, which means he's happy, and we gather friends of his is in them cars.

"We stop to take on water. 'You wait for me,' he says, and out he piles and runs ahead and as he passes down that siding the doors and windows of them house cars blooms out with shouting heads faster than ever Philadelphy done that time for Paul Revere.

"They gathers and swallers him up, those folks, and he's gone away indoors into the middle of their Christmas.

"Up ahead old eng-*ine* puffs a couple of quick rings and back comes the whistle floating. She's just at sunset and the day is square ahead, shining down the train, and makes the branches of that lone tree sparkle and shimmy, and all the world look good. You can see the elbow and half-a-head and shoulder of the engineer, leanin' out, drawin' a bead down the line, and just ahead over the rise is Sherman Hill and old Cheyenne.

"We starts to roll. We passes by the siding and the house-cars with their washing strung between, their ladder-steps and toys of kids laid in the dust, new that morning. Inside there's music.

"As we commence to roll, them cars slips back-ards faster, like a passing train, and no Rodriguez. Then a door breaks open—here he comes, a demijohn under one arm, running sidewise for to catch the smiles, but he's got so much to say, so many hands to wave, that he don't make much time.

"Such a yapping and a yow-yowing as went up! They *wouldn't* let him go. They took after him, young 'uns and them as weren't too drunk, some cute little gals, too, and "Rodriguez!" was the cry and it went up to heaven. I don't know what that guy had done, but it must have been something awful good.

"Now he come about to the coupling of our car, still so full of merry Christmas he couldn't quit and get aboard. He commenced the exhibition of us—me and Hank and Lemmy settin' in the door—speeling off about us with one hand, all in Mexican. '*Amigos, amigos muy buenos* oy-oy!' and wavin' the demijohn till you'd of thought we was the finest people in the world and he'd never had a friend until he met us.

"We set there, three big old sillies in the door, and took that jabber; I bet we could have got elected king of that place in half-a-minute if we'd got down.

"However it was the actions of the demijohn concerned us most; we hollered at Rodriguez to cut the conversation and get aboard.

"He poured it on and got within a step or two and then the damndest thing happened I ever seen. A woman run out of the last car holding up the tiniest, brownest baby that ever God give to the Mexicans. It done something to Rodriguez. That gentleman laid down his demijohn, reached in his pocket, and pulled out one of them toy auto-*mo*-biles three inches long you buy at the five-and-ten. '*Nacimiento*!' he hollers till the siding rings, and pitches his automobile to the young woman.

"Then he comes our way and how he travels, how he packs that demijohn! He'd have made a big name for himself playing football at some college, but now he's lost two cars and can't make up. He comes as far as our rear coupling and can't gain any more. The nose of the freight is over the hill.

"Lemmy Sykes stands up in the doorway, both hands open to Rodriguez for a forward pass. That Mexican took time to grin. Then with a twist and little dance in the air he lets the demijohn come flying, straight to Lemmy, and we had her safe aboard. He run easy then and was really making that freight car travel backwards when I remembers myself and shuts the door. '*A-migos!*' he hollers. Son-of-a-bitch but we laughed—'*a-MIGOS!*' Even with the door shut, rattling down the hill we heard him for a long time: *Amigos!* Finally he died out.

"Well, that trip we rolled happy. Our song was some-no pain, went and looked up Rosita and Maria and thing to hear. For supper we was at Cheyenne feeling they weren't hard to take at all, after we'd told 'em about our friend Rodriguez, how he'd been delayed, you know, met some gals along the line; and Christmas night don't wait on any man. Son-of-a-bitch, we had ourselves a time.

"Old Cheyenne's all right, but not for long. We'd hid the demijohn, figuring it good insurance till we found a better climate.

"Going to Salt Lake we finished her, and when we got inside the yards we never noticed, we was all so warm and nice. Spent the night right there, thinking because the place is flat it must be a desert; woke up stiff as boards and seen the sun rise white over the Wasatch back of town."

Happy Jack coughed and spat till he made our stove sizzle. "One more clean shirt," he said, "and it's Alberkerky for me. Yeah," he said, "spotted up a lung that night in old Salt Lake; 'course I didn't start the bad spot there, started one time I accidentally got into Arkansas and being a sociable sort indulged me in some conversation. But them Arkansawyers! . . . They can say more before breakfast than you'd care to hear. Strained me wind a little but otherwise than that I come away in honorable condition."

"You son-of-a-gun," said Jody, "I wish't you'd died there; we'd put you in the ground to make corn grow."

"Now *Jody*! . . ." said Jack.

"Ever get to Alberkerky?" said Cherokee.

"Never did," said Jack. "Some way it happened I ended up that trip in Spokane, Washington, and got me married."

"The hell!" said Cherokee.

"Yeah," said Jack, "it's a fact; women finds me quite desirable. You know—"

"Tell your lie," said Cherokee.

" 'Tain't no lie," said Jack. "Doggone you, you hurt my feelings—she was the woman I loved. Sure, Irene was all right; it was her mammy made the difference. Met 'em both the same night. Danced twice with Irene and asks her how she's going home. 'On the street-car,' she says. 'No, you're not,' I says, 'I'm taking you.' 'Oh, no,' she says, 'I'm here with my mother.' It ended by the three of us driving home together.

"And you know, next two times I took her out her mammy come along. 'Well,' I says to myself, 'here really is a nice girl.'

"We made it fine until one thing happened," said Jack, and he began to bounce his silver bullet again. "I give that little gal the best years o' my life, forty bucks a week, radios, Simmons beds—everything a woman's heart desires. And everything was hunky-dory till one day Ma, she asks me conversational-like how I come to have this here scar across't my cheek. I tells her. 'Jack Patee!' she says. 'Why, you're nothing but a common *bum!*'

"After that, every time I took my hat she'd ask me

where I was going. Yeah, I'm telling you, it got so bad I couldn't even go to the toilet without I told that lady first.

"One day I give it up—just packed my duds and left.

"I've thought considerable on that mistake I made and figured some way it was this," and Jack held up the silver bullet. "Here's the reason: at Toledo I never kept a-goin' like I should; I set on my foundations, got a scar and a story to tell I don't conceal, being a honest man. But it just goes to show how a feller's life catches up on him."

The one o'clock whistle blew and Jack let his big fat hand swallow the bullet and slide it back into his pocket.

We took our lunch pails and went outside. The fog had rolled in thick. Dark shapes of trucks stood in it and men moved shadow-like. The cry of geese came falling through the mist and we could hear the fog horns mourning faintly on the river as though somewhere far away some one had died and the fog buried him. Then the motors started.

I rode down in Jody's truck with Happy Jack, three in the front seat.

"Let me see that bullet," Jody said, and Happy Jack handed it over across me. Jody took one hand off the wheel and because it was dark inside the cab he leaned toward the window to read the Mexican inscription on the fat end. And then it happened. Red Killiam, mill boss, pulled out his pick-up truck from Office Alley. I yelled; Jody grabbed the wheel. For just a second the bullet balanced on the window sill; then it toppled over and made a silver tinkle on the runningboard—that was all.

"Hey Jody, hold up!" said Jack.

We stopped and he got out, walked back there in the mist, and we could barely see him on his knees, face in the mud, dodging the other trucks as they whined past.

Jody started out.

"Hey Jody!" Jack called, "wait a minute; where you going?"

"Alberkerky," said Jody, and gunned away.

Jack came walking into the mill at one forty-five. He had not found his bullet and he caught hell from the boss. Furthermore, somewhere earlier, he had caught a cold, a bad one, that settled in his lungs. And because he had a bad spot there, it went deeper down with every breath. By Tuesday he had pneumonia. Friday he was dead. We buried him the morning after New Year's in the graveyard up at Bird Town.

JIM MAGEE'S SAND

THE year Achilles hit 110 and Masterson Securities refinanced and came out with some gilt edge debentures at 6½, the year the wind of Pelican Island blew his cattle into the sea and Melanie Jones danced in a meat market and Uncle Arky Billy fought the Duke, T. S. Ordway attended one meeting too many. It didn't happen all at once; it was gradual business, building up and building up until all of a sudden he was absentee and we didn't see him any more around the El Dorado Investment Company.

All we got was word of him—by phone, by wire—though sometimes on the summer evenings, if you walked alone from the bunkhouse among the pens of cattle when the light blew in low from the bay over ripe grain, you would hear the soft crunch and mutter of a heavy car, and a big Lincoln would slide past and give you just a whiff of good cigars and the glimpse and echo of big things in the making—those little words that break the ground before ever the boys in the bunk-house take their picks and go to work.

However, word or man, the cattle in the pens continued to grow fat, and the grain prospered, and if you had flown the plane that comes over every afternoon at four, nine minutes out of San Francisco for New York, you would have seen the feed-yard down below like a dark red stain on the earth. You would have seen the arm of the slough reaching among the cattle, and the ribbon of the river end and frazzle out among the delta islands to make a bay.

We had a lot of rain that year. It began early in December, raining four or five days a week, and by Christmas we were watching the river and the levees. The yards turned to gray paste that oozed away in layers down the alleys. The cattle stopped eating and stood all day huddled against the fences where the rain drifted them. Men and dogs got up early and stayed wet, and three times every week T. S. Ordway telephoned from El Paso where he'd traveled on a deal to get some Mexican cattle shipped across the border, and to buy and sell a couple of banks in his spare time.

So it was the morning before New Year's when Barb, my chunky sorrel, and I turned down Mill Alley square into a southeast gale that humped our backs worse than it did the cattle's, and blew a thin rain up the slough. Outside the bay was choppy.

Jim Magee's Sand

We stopped on the knoll above the beet-pulp pit, which looks like a stadium filled with stale shredded cocoanut, warm and steaming, and watched a dragline crane bucketing the pulp from a barge that was tied in the slough against the pit. Down there in the alley stood a black pick-up truck, which meant only one thing: trouble and Jim Magee. Those two went together. Whenever anything got wrong, you sent for the scavenger bunch, and first Jim would come in his black pick-up, an omen of disaster, and then his crew of roustabouts and handy-men—all ages, shapes, and sizes—perched like a flock of vultures around the edge of a flat-bed truck. There wasn't anything they couldn't do, with Jim to lead. He was Ordway's construction foreman, black Irish, six feet long and two feet wide—a carpenter, blacksmith, mechanic, plumber, even a shipwright, for he had worked in the Navy Yard and knew all about boats and how to caulk and repair barges. And so he had charge of the giant crane and the four Company barges that hauled beet-pulp night and day. All the water pipes on the ranch were laid by Jim and dug up by him when they leaked, and only he knew where the mains ran under the ground and which valve to turn when you wanted the water shut off in Mill Alley.

Barb and I went down Mill Alley, cutting the wind, and got about even with the truck when up came Jim himself through one of the holes in the side of the pit where men go down to the drains at the bottom. He lay flat again and began lifting on something just out of sight that was a little too much for him. I got off and lent a hand and we lifted out one of those Jaeger pumps that push the rain and beat juice out of the pit.

"What's the trouble?" I said.

"Carburetor cracked," said Jim, pointing—that hand was knotty-red and the arm brown and hard as the bole of a tree. Jim wore what he did every day: shirtsleeves, brown canvas breeches tucked in knee-boots, and a rain hat that was extra. Also he had something he never went without: a ball-peen hammer slung through a loop on his trouser-leg. I wondered how he had got the pump up thirty feet from the bottom of the pit, because it was a fair weight for two men.

"Feeling kind of waspy today?" I asked.

"Yeah," said Jim, looking right at me with those bare blue eyes so that I never could tell whether he wanted to laugh or fight. "Yeah," he said, "these days whenever it rains, I eat an extra plate of beans," and he gave a wave behind him toward the river. I knew he meant the levees. T. S. hadn't doctored them this autumn as he should. He had meant to; Jim had been after him about it, and T. S. had hell here once before, years ago—1918, I think it was—when the sky broke open for a whole month and the river ran and his was the only levee to hold. He did it then himself—skinned a six-mule team—with baled hay rustled from the warehouse. But that was years ago when T. S. didn't have so many meetings.

"When is it due?" I asked Jim. I meant the tide. Along

near Christmas when the days are shortest and the moon a certain way, something happens to the tides, and if they back up in the bay against a southeast wind and the river is coming down, then watch out.

"'Bout five," said Jim. "Four fifty-five, I think. Let's have a look now and see how she stands."

We took off around the end of the pit and came along the dock where the dragline engine roared and the wind howled through the planking and nearly blew us off into the slough. We hung over the side and saw a big white ruler fastened to one of the piles, where the water stood above the number "7."

"She's ebbing now!" screamed Jim.

She would be in at five—nine-feet-six, the highest of the year.

We looked down past the mill where the angle of the levee fringed with tules held six thousand head of cattle between the slough and the river.

"I don't like it," said Jim; and then: "Ever buckaroo on water?"

"What do you mean?" I said.

"Swim?" said Jim.

"Come on," I said, "*come* on! . . ."

"You goddamned cowboys got a barge of cattle coming this afternoon, feeder steers from Mandeville."

"Well?" I said.

"Well, hell," said Jim. "I canceled my pulp barges today; you let yours get away early and we can't catch her now."

I looked at the slough. "You mean a barge won't fit in here this afternoon?"

"I mean that," said Jim. "And if a barge does, chances are the river will too. . . . But," he said, "they're your cattle, not mine. I'm not cattle boss, am I?"

"You son-of-a-gun," I said, "you're vice-president around here and you know it."

Jim gave me a shrug and a gesture of the hands that passed all title to the howling wind and the water rising in the slough. "We don't need a vice-president," he said. "We need a levee."

And then he struck off along the dock to see what Big Bill Williams was doing with the dragline.

At noon we heard the river was three feet above flood at Pride's Landing; at one o'clock she hit Brownsville and ran over, and they opened the Battle Island by-pass to save the levees lower down.

Midway on our afternoon round, with the wind sharpening all the time and the rain beginning to feel like pellets of lead, Barb and I met Jacks in Office Alley. He told me to get wire-cutters from Tony at the shop and to go to the river and stand by in case we had to take the cattle out in a hurry.

When I crossed the knoll above the mill, I could barely see the river through the rain—an ugly swollen thing like a big brown arm that's got infected. The open two or three miles to the Appleton short was lathered into whitecaps all the way, looking more like blood than water. Six thousand cattle were a reddish smear and Jim Magee's men black dots scrambling around in the mud.

A truck passed loaded with sand; then two more full of light gravel.

I turned into Long Alley, which runs between pens for a mile and a half to the river. Over on the levee men were keeping out the slough with shovels. You could hear them shouting faintly as though they were a mile away instead of a hundred yards.

Away down at the elbow of the levee, where the slough opens off the river, a bulldozer tractor was stuck; and when I got closer, I saw Jim Magee was there and Jacks and Dynamite, my pard. Waves smashed over them high as a house, but nobody minded the river. A muddy line of men was passing bags of sand for fifty yards along the slough, like an old-fashioned bucket brigade, to a low place where already a lake of water had seeped through into the pens. Others filled the bags as fast as trucks could bring the sand. Every able-bodied man was on that levee.

The cattle stood around and watched, in water over their knees and very serious and quiet, like a lot of sober old veterans.

The waves were sending spray in jets and gobs and forked tongues like white fire; it mixed with the rain and wind and hit those little men around the bulldozer so hard they seemed to be sewed up in a white border of some kind. Jim had another tractor, a big RD-7, on the end of the bulldozer and a couple of trucks rigged in tandem by their chains; and when he gave the signal all that line of metal went to pulling like a big freight does on a hill, and out came the bulldozer like a rabbit from a hollow log and ran on backwards fifteen yards before Jim could get her stopped.

Just then I bumped into Dynamite in a Company raincoat about thirteen sizes too large, that dragged the ground as he walked.

"Hey!" he shouted; his face was very red from the rain. "She's a rip-snorter and a vinegar-roan! Why didn'tcha bring a boat?"

A wave came over, blotting him out, making the ground shudder and go down and up, like a man hit hard on the jaw.

"We're hopin' the jelly will hold!" sang Dynamite. "It was only T.S. put her here; looks like God Almighty'll take her away!"

Then out of all the time in the world, one of those things happened that sometimes does: the grandfather of every wave that ever rose hit that river levee and I'm telling you it rocked the cattle on their feet. I started to run; I thought I saw the ocean coming. Dynamite started, too; but when he saw me, he stopped and began laughing; and then the wave came down out of the sky with a slap and knocked him flat and sent him skidding up the alley like a log on a beach.

It left him and went back, and with it a big chunk of the levee.

Jim Magee was just unhitching his bulldozer over on

the slough. He never made a sign; just got aboard and came our way, dodging around his own black pick-up and peeling off the levee with him and leaving it in the hole—just a morsel for the next big wave to tear away. But he came again, and with him boards and barrels and the trash of twenty years collected on that levee—some old gray bales of hay that looked as if they'd been there since T. S. Ordway stopped the river back in '18.

He took time to stop the sand trucks coming down Long Alley and made them dump their loads and sent them back for heavy gravel. Then he really went to skinning that cat; he slung mud from those flying tracks farther than the river spray and faster, till he was beating those big rollers to every punch and the cut in the levee began to heal.

Half an hour and he had her done, spun the big cat on a dime, flirting its tail at the river, and rattled over to the slough. He'd never bothered his men at all; they'd wasted time just watching.

It was getting dark. Dynamite and I hurried to the levee to see Jacks, while the wind smacked our clothes against our skin and took our breath away and kept shoving in those ugly brown rollers as though it wanted to finish us off before dark.

Jacks said wait a while about the cattle, the Old Man was coming. I never blamed him; six thousand head of cattle are not easily moved in the first place, get clear off feed when they are, and lose pounds and time and money—all that in addition to the mix-up. So we waited.

Four-twenty, it was, when Dynamite nudged my arm and I saw a long black limousine slide down the alley—a Lincoln, which meant only one thing: T. S. Ordway himself. The chauffeur didn't know us but we got a wave from old T.S. He always had a word for the boys; he was good at words, that old operator.

Jim Magee was busy but Jacks gathered around; and even old Reuben Child, the lame cowboy, who never missed a doings that had cattle in it, came hobbling on his cane out of the dusk.

T.S. didn't leave the car. It wasn't like him. Years ago he would have been out there lending a hand on the levee, skinning a pair of mules himself, putting muscle as well as words into it; but the years had gone and left him at his desk with a paunch, a little sag around the corners of his face, gray hair, glasses, plenty of good clothes.

He held a meeting at the window of the car and its matter was simply this: Cattle in or out. Old Rube began to wave his cane after a spell and you could tell where he stood, but the others knew better; they outvoted him and the cattle stayed.

Fifteen minutes and the tide would start downhill. Maybe on paper it looked all right, but outdoors it's different. You can't tell all the things a southeast wind can do in fifteen minutes when there's a river and a tide to help.

I'm here to say the wrath of God came down to earth that quarter-hour in December, 1940. First, lightning broke the sky and came into our valley and even the rain stood still. For a second you could see a hundred miles and everything was stuck, jaundiced, the hills shrunk. You didn't want to look, but you had to. Night fell on one gust of wind. Then everything got bigger. Those little three-inch waves lapping in the slough, where all the storm couldn't reach, were big enough to sink a house. They were the tide. Like death, you couldn't see it. There was only one wind on earth and one river and one human being which was you—nobody else mattered.

I had tied my pony. He reared now and broke away and ran off up the alley; it was time to run.

You just could see the line of men along the slough, with weather passing in between so fast that that muddy line seemed hardly to move. It looked slow, a thousand miles away, but it moved, it had life; and all the wind in the sky and all the rivers of earth couldn't stop those Okies, Arkies, Dutchmen, and Swedes. . . . They stayed with her, though if you'd asked them why, they couldn't have said. It wasn't for T. S. Ordway, not altogether for Jim Magee—just to win. And they fought and scrambled and slung those bags until lights moved upstream on the water.

"She's here!" somebody screamed.

I looked and looked till the wind stung shut my eyes. When I opened them, there was the shadow of the cattle barge, like a dark building two stories high, and ahead of it one hawser-length the tiny shadow of the tug. Red and green lights were on its deck house. Now and then a wave building up in shore would put them out completely.

T.S. and Jacks broke out of the Lincoln at a run.

We followed.

Jim Magee, coming from the left, met us at the elbow of the levee where the slough takes off the river.

"Jim!" said old T.S., "we can't have that barge in here; she'll flood the yards. I telephoned from Stockton for a motor barge to stop her. . . . Jim, I want you to send a boat out and tell the captain he can't come in here!"

I looked at the river and felt a little sick at my stomach.

Jim didn't have an answer.

We stood there in the rain, leaning forward as if we could see better that way and think better, and you could feel the seconds going by, the motion of that storm and water and the barge coming down so fast.

One of Jim's boys splashed up out of the dark, said something, and Jim repeated at a yell, "Mr. Ordway, did you hear that? She's over now. . . . The slough is over now in a place sixty feet wide!"

This time T.S. didn't have an answer.

From faraway there came the snort of cattle, sharp, anxious—the one they make, not when they're playing or hungry, but only when they've nosed into something strange they don't like. I could see the dark water creeping out around their feet as clearly as if I'd been right there. T.S. started: "Jim . . ." But Jim had spun away into the night.

We tried to see where he went and ended up looking in each other's faces.

The tug was edging for the slough, quartering the gale, and T.S. sounded like a man about to die when he said, too quietly, "Funny he doesn't use his searchlight."

Was she coming or was she not? In that pale shimmery light that darkness brings over water you could see the barge clearly for a second, stuck in such cross-currents of wind and tide, crested with so much white foam, that she seemed to move hardly at all. Then she blotted out. It became plain she wasn't coming for the slough; she had passed the turning and was headed on straight down.

Old Rube said: "Bless me, gracious!"

T.S. kept his opinion.

We couldn't figure where the barge would land. As we wondered she started swinging off-shore, square into the wind, straight across the flood and incoming tide; and when the wind took her she stopped still and that tug on the end of its chain leaped and staggered like a dog chained to a wall. Then slowly, little by little, it crept ahead.

The last we saw, the barge lay off into the southeast like a sunken reef, with the spray arching clear over her and the Appleton shore three miles away.

"Well," said T.S., and swallowed his upper lip, "there

goes three hundred head of yearling steers somewhere. They're not ours till they're on the dock; that's the agreement." He and Jacks discussed the barge company, the amount of insurance it usually carried; and suddenly they remembered the break in the slough levee and called for Jim Magee; but there was no Jim. They discussed, waited, finally started out.

Far up the river lights came back. In a minute she was plainly seen—tug and barge riding the wind, heading for the slough's mouth as fast as the gusts of rain.

"It's the barge," said T.S.

"By God it is," said Jacks.

"It's the barge all right," said Old Rube.

"No searchlight," said T.S. "I don't understand . . ." but he never finished that one. I didn't let him. The sneaking hunch had taken me that no captain of any cattle barge on earth could snake his load in blind out of that kind of river that time of night. If he had a light, where was it? I looked behind and then I hollered: "The pick-up! Watch the pick-up!" Jim was signaling; his lights blinked on and off.

T.S. started for him at a run.

The barge was at the mouth of the slough.

"Jim!" The wind brought it back to us diluted "*Jim!* . . ."

The barge was in.

Jim moved the pick-up to keep his lights in view and T.S., who was beating on the glass, slipped and went flat in the mud.

Jacks ran to pick him up and Dynamite and I took off along the levee.

Once the barge hit the far side and stuck a minute; we gained and got ahead.

She wasn't fifty feet away.

We heard the water gurgling at the break as Jim overtook us.

His men were there, still trying, wading in the dark apron of water that slid over into the pens, plopping down, one at a time, sacks that made splashes like pebbles thrown into the sea.

"We're gonna moor the barge across the gap," sang Jim. "Grab the forward line and tie to as many fence posts as you can."

Even in the dark you could hear the mutter of dissent: "What the hell now? Magee's gone nuts!"

"Watch out!" yelled Jim. "Watch out for the big wave."

The barge loomed over us in the night, big as a battleship, and a wave we never saw knocked us to our knees. Then she hit with a thud and stuck. Dynamite had a line and was looping it on one fence post, then a second, then a third, before she loosened in the mud and slid ahead, and the first post came up stickily like a tooth being pulled. But the tug was churning on the off-side and we had her fast against the bank.

This was good, but not enough. Thirty feet of water slid past the stern and over into the pens, faster and faster in the narrow space, and the sand was far away.

Jim began wading out. He tripped once and I thought he had washed away into the pens, or had sunk down into the mud—that levee's full of holes—but he made a quick stagger and got through.

Then he was gone and we had the water.

Sammy King came up, Jim's straw boss, and half a dozen men with bags of sand. The water on that thirty feet was knee deep, but it might have been a hundred. We threw in bags and boards and mud, handfuls of tules, but it all went away with the dark water and you could hear the bags go splash and tumble down beyond, into the pens, and the sloshing of the cattle moving with them. We went in shoulder to shoulder, hand to hand, making the water break around us, slapping at that dark apron with our boards and shovels. I saw the water find a hole and rim it out and suck into it with a sound like a man strangling to death, until that little hole became a pit and then a gash and then a ragged wound in the side of the levee.

Sammy King and another guy and I joined hands and went down in up to our knees, then our thighs, but the ground slid away under us and they hauled us out spitting sand and water, damning.

We saw two figures coming—Jacks and old T.S.

"Stay with her, boys," the Old Man said. "Stay with her now, you've got her!"

We cussed him under our breath.

Something moved and slipped in the darkness overhead, along the deck of the barge, and came on over into the water with a sucking splash. I thought it was a bag of sand; when the ripples quieted, I saw it was a yearling steer.

The tug had got its searchlight going. The big beam came to us in blinding yellow stripes and flashes, across the rain, through the railings of the barge as the tug rocked on the water. You could see the beeves stowed in like sacks, gray and muddy, and the deckhand crouching by the capstan pulling something, all come and gone in a flash; and then there was another figure, a great big shadow of a guy standing among the cattle with a hammer, a heavy ball-peen hammer, smacking out their brains as though they were so many ten-penny nails.

"Why, he's killing the cattle!" said T.S. and just stood there.

Then we got busy.

We caught those yearling steers and laid them in the gap; we poured and filled them in like mortar between the barge and the levee. We were masons that night—stonemasons who worked in flesh—and we built a wall such as no men ever built before. It was like the Bible's description of the last great battle of the world, when the living shall walk upon the dead, because many of those steers Jim hadn't killed, and they died slowly till we found them.

We used our bars and shovels. You'd go along and feel the ground move under you and that would be a muscle dying, a hind-leg usually. Once I put my foot into a hole and went down deep in something warm, and as I rose part of the ground came with me like a shadow. There was a shape there worse than death—horns and eyes and blood and mud. It moved. I had a shovel with me; I smashed it down and got it under water, but it came again and I had to smash and trample till the apron of the break ran smooth.

Like bricks we added them and stuck our bars and shovels in behind for piling, and our knees, till the pressure of the flood grew weaker and the wall could stand alone.

Things moved fast. We got to talking short and silly as men do sometimes when they've got a lot to win. "Pass the sirloin, Johnny!" was the word for more beef on the line; and "Jim Magee's sand" was another—"Magee's sand, worth fifty bucks a bag!" And so it came to be known through all the West wherever men knew a horse from a cow, and that's a lot of country.

After I don't know how long, Sammy King called to Jim to hold it.

Far to the north thunder was growling as though it still wanted to come back and get us. We could hear the cattle in the pens still going with the water. But no more water would come; we'd rolled up that apron.

We stood around tamping down a little and filling in, knowing we had done something big and getting ready to tell each other about it, but still relishing the story in our minds. Before we'd decided on just the right words, Jim Magee came along the levee, dark in his rainclothes, narrow at the top and wide at the bottom like the shape of a tree. He came on one side, Ordway and Jacks stood on the other; and of us all that had been thinking of good words only T.S. found any to say. "Jim!" he pealed out, "Jim boy, that was a fine piece of work, a great piece of work. Here, let's have a drink on it!"

He brought out a silver pocket flask, undid the cork, and passed it across to Jim.

Magee looked like a kid at Christmas time who's been handed a great big expensive toy he doesn't want. He knocked his hat back with one hand, raised the flask with the other, then brought the first hand down and wiped off the nozzle; then he pulled. The flask went round the circle and back to old T.S., but by that time it was empty.

Nobody has thought of just the right word, although it's quiet now, the wind and rain having gone away with the thunder. A flash comes all of a sudden from the tug's searchlight and T.S. is cut out of the darkness and given to us to remember, standing there alone all sopped and muddy, with an empty flask. He's on one side; on the other are we and Jim.

"Well," says Argo, the radical Slav, the one we call "Communeeste," "well, by God, I guess that's her!" and reaches into his shirt pocket for a cigarette.

WOMEN AND DYNAMITE

EVERY winter day at one o'clock Dynamite and I took heavy six-tined forks that were meant to shovel feed for cattle and cleaned the barn, leaving our horses saddled in their stalls, ready for the afternoon round. This was a day that sometimes in a California winter blows like a blessing from the sea. Dynamite that very morning had put on long underwear, expecting a cold snap, and as he warmed up a little at the end of the fork and began to sweat, the wool tickled his skin and made him itch and swear and blame his wife.

"Woman is a weak-minded outfit, anyway," he said, boosting a load out the window to the compost pile and grinning his little boy's grin. For a lad of twenty-six with a wife and four children, Dynamite had a lot to say. "Never did use undy-wear," he said, "till I got married, nor socks neither. Back home when it come cold we put old newspaper down our boots; they's all a man needs till he gets a woman."

Home for Dynamite was any place he happened to be. Once it had been the Utah border, once the Oregon cattle country. . . .

We worked in shadow. Sea wind blowing in the open door swept dust over us from the gray dirt floor of the barn. Outside, trucks were passing on the road; we could see the backs of cattle in their pens beyond, and then the deep adobe fields, tinged by early rains with a faint green shadow of new grass. Far away the Napa Hills rose up and made a line across the open door just even with the stirrup of the boss's saddle, hanging on its peg.

"All right," I heard Dynamite mutter, "here he is."

Jacks, the foreman, stood in the lighted square of doorway—or rather the outline of him; you couldn't see his face, only the light that ran forward along the brim of his hat and in the folds of his overall pants. The Napa Hills cut across him waist high.

He stuck a hand in each hip pocket, rocked a minute on his heels, and told us there was a bulling steer in Pen 81 that ought to come out. Then he went away.

We forked out several loads.

"Notice Jacks there?" said Dynamite, and I could tell he had something on his mind. "Looked pretty big, didn't he?"

I said I guessed he had. But he *had* looked big; I remembered how the Napa Hills came only to his waist.

"He ain't that big though," said Dynamite; "it was just the light made him look thataway."

I agreed.

"And did ye ever notice him there—till he talks he's awful good. He's maybe coming to say you got a raise, or to give ye the day off. You can't tell."

Dynamite with an idea was like a chicken with a seed, taking it up, dropping it, clucking over it several times, and finally either swallowing it or walking away. But if ever he took a thing, it went all the way down; and then the words came tumbling out and spread away over the plain, like his own Colorado River.

Now all this sounded like a big seed, so I waited, and in a minute he said, "See this barn?" He was standing at the window, leaning on his fork, looking out across the compost pile. I came along and pitched a load and said yes, I did see the barn.

"Sure pretty, ain't it?" said Dynamite.

Well, it did look pretty. It stood off there half a mile away across a grassy field that was so thin and green it looked like water, and the wind ran on it sparkling. The barn was part in shadow, part in sun; and somebody had cut three black squares out of its side that were windows, like ours, and on a hill beyond there was a mist as in the spring.

"Yessir," said Dynamite, "that's a fine idee of what a barn should be. Makes you want to git up and start over there, don't it? . . . thinkin' there is all that makes a good barn good—sweet hay and horses in their stalls, pussycats, saddles, old harness hangin', smellin' like last summer. You say, 'By God, that must be the best barn in all the world,' but it ain't, is it?"

"I don't know," I said, "maybe it is."

"Till you get there anyway, it is," said Dynamite, and then he said no more and I didn't hurry him.

We took our ponies and started on the afternoon round, going first to get the bulling steer and putting him in the hospital. That brought us out on Mill Alley between the pens of cattle, on a knoll above the mill where the wind of forty miles strikes bare and always blows. It took the feed-grains from the mangers and stuck them in our eyes and slopped them through our clothes and curled the dust away on a long banner from the ventilator on top of the mill.

Dynamite pulled up his pony.

"Hear it?" he said.

"Hear what?" I said.

"That's what it is," said Dynamite. "Damn me, if it ain't!"

He held his hat on with one hand, looking right up at the sky where some power lines crossed going to the mill. "Don'tcha *hear* it?" he said.

I said, "What the devil are you talking about?"

"The wind in the wires," said Dynamite.

"What about it?" I said.

"Nothing," said Dynamite. "Nothing about *it*, but about me, plenty; 'cause that's the sound I heard the night of the twentieth September, '33, when I rode off the top o' the world to have a drink and see my girl."

We went on down the knoll and around the hay field to the big stack, where the wind couldn't find us, nor the boss, and there Dynamite told me his story.

"Every year in May we took cattle on the mountain—earlier sometimes, if the year was good—and always we was champing to get away. Winter in town leaves a feller in the red. Bills here, argy-ments here, some little maiden a-wanting to git married—they's no profit. You go along with your feet fixed one way and your mind another and if ye get as far as March without meeting the sheriff on the way, you're lucky. March—she's better than a drink of whiskey! Then your ponies' hair begins to slip, you're getting out the pack saddles, a-oiling up old leather, and every guy is friendly again for the first time since Christmas.

"We hit the Mormon trail that comes in out o' the desert and takes up past town onto the mountain. Our range was all that as was east of west and north of south, and any more we needed. That country's not like this; we don't prison our cattle. The rim-rocks is our fences.

"Well, when you first go up she's hunky-dory. The cattle wants to go, the ponies wants to go—they's sick of valley living. All you're cravin' is that feel of hair between your knees and a chance to run and bust him out; you look the other way just a-hoping that pa'tic'lar red steer with the Roman nose and the droop-horn will take a break, 'cause you see he's got a run in him, and sure enough he does and then you make old mountain smoke.

"My job was what they call the Tennessee Pass, where cattle drifts in summer when the meadow feed goes short, and sometimes they travels all of Eighty Mile Hill clear down to the river, unless I catch 'em first, which I usually does.

"I made lone camp on Aspen Creek, by a big old boulder where there was a cedar tree and a ice cold spring run out of the stone. I made me seats and tables, a corral built of them hairy cedar logs; a bed of boughs; a canvas lean-to for when it rained. I packed in grain for my pony. I had horseshoes, nails, and pounds and pounds of sowbelly, spuds, and beans; and I had all my thoughts of what'd been since last I camped on Aspen Crick. To think 'em I had company. Off south was the Old Man, twelve thousand feet and white with snow all summer long. I could see him there on moonlight nights, hanging off above me like a ghost. I'd sit by the fire then, eating my beans, pounding me some jerky for a stew, and when I had eat, I'd go on sitting there just to listen—me all alone, you know, and old pony over there in his corral a-munchin'. I'd watch the firelight run up and down a grove of quakies—quaking aspens, that growed beside the water, thin and white, you know, with del-y-cate leaves like they was people's hair. I'd imagine they *was* people. It was so awful quiet there, seemed like I had a chance to think for the first time; and them little trees put me in mind of fellers I knowed. When you was a kid, did you ever sit and think who was your best friends? Well, that's what I done. I'm not ashamed to own it. I wasn't no more 'n seventeen, anyways. . . . So I thought of Hap, my pard, who'd been with me through many a scrape and was keepin' my other horse, a little sorrel with cat hips. I thought a lot about that cat-hipped sorrel. I needed him to spell old Tony off, and hoped that Hap would take a notion to ride up and see me. Then I thought of Kitty McWilliams and Hoopaloo, both good guys, and of a feller named Harry I met that winter. "Handsome Harry," they called him, and he was drunk—drunk all the time. Once he was a-gonna meet us at a certain place but never showed, and they found him two days later on the Della Road, froze stiff, drunk. Cedar Bill, I thought about, and others, but amongst them aspen trees was one smaller than the rest, with branches like the arms of ferns, and leaves the wind whispered through and made to dance in the firelight, and that one was my girl, Maxine."

Dynamite put a straw into his mouth and seemed to think of something off the path of his story.

"But that's all right," he said, "thas-all-right. I had a good time there three months, and then I began to tire. You get so used to yourself. Everything's right where you left it. In the morning you go out and at evening you come back and if a squirrel has walked across the table and kicked at the crumbs, you'd know it. And I got tired of hearing nobody's voice but my own, and tired of working with horseflesh and cowflesh and rope and leather, and tired as hell of eatin' alone. I wanted to mix with human kind.

"And so it was this night . . . I'd been out late. There was a change in the weather coming. I could see the sun go down orange out here in Californy, and I guessed that might mean trouble for cowboys. This was late September, see, and by then anything can happen. If snow comes, cattle drift, and you drift with 'em, whether it's a mile or eighty. So I'd made a long round and come out just at evening on the Indian Rock. I could see all the valley, all the desert, all the mountain. Oh, she was a panoramic! Old Tony and I set there and watched her, while down in the valley the lights come on one by one, like little stars. A cluster of 'em made the town; one I knowed was the café my girl Maxine worked, and I wanted to be there awful bad. Now that town didn't amount to *nuthin'!* Why, at high noon it wouldn't make a shadow, and dry, O Jesus! No water run by that place! . . . I don't know why I wanted to go; I'd lived there all my life, but I had to go.

"I says to Tony, 'How do you feel?' and he says, 'Fine.' So we piles over the edge.

"I knowed I could make it in three hours going straight down and be there before them little stars went out. I'd go right to the café and see Maxine; I'd find Hap and get my sorrel horse, and I'd do a lot of things that would be worth telling later.

"Did ye ever start to go anywheres at night? The

how nor why of it don't matter, ye just go. Well, that was the way with me; and I begun to sing, because I was a silly kid then. I sung that song—you've heard me:

> *Up*-on my pony,
> *Up*-on old Tony,
> To ride o'er the prairie
> To see my charming Mary. . . .

"And so I slid off that mountain and I bet I was something to hear. That country's funny built. She's made of sandstone and looks like somebody threw her up on edge, like a deck of cards. Just when I was flyin' high, one of them cards slipped out from under old Tony, and to me it felt like the whole deck. We just quit the ground and flew a ways, and when we come down I was pinned agin a cedar tree, under the saddle, with old Tony waving his feet at the moon and me a-spittin' sandstone and trying to git a-hold of his head. See, I had one leg under the saddle and agin the tree, and every time he'd move I'd think that leg was goin' with him.

"We man-o-veered round a bit, and I got my short tug on the off-side undone, and the saddle slid ahead and let me go. Well, that was all right. My leg was still there, and pretty quick we was on our way down the mountain. I was feeling no pain; I couldn't do wrong. Did ye ever feel that way? . . . Go through a narrer escape and come out knowing the angels was on your side and you couldn't miss from there on in? I went down that mountain, under them big pines, and I was light enough to fly. I was a-gonna see my girl; I was a-gonna have a drink and put my feet under a table and have people bring me things. And I didn't care how long it took, 'cause I had music in me and could have rid to the end of the world.

"The old night opened up and let me down like water does a stone. Air rushin' in my ears was all I heard. I'd watch them little lights go flicker through the trees. They'd been at my feet to start, but now they was pushing away into the desert and I spurred old Tony to catch 'em. I got thinking of Maxine at the café. She'd be off at nine. By then my leg would be all swole up and sore, and maybe she'd take me home and rub liniment on it. I'd have a bath first. I knowed a place I could git one for thirty-five cents. They give you medicated soap, too. And then I thought of Hap, my pal, and where I could find him. Probably the Hearty Laugh Saloon; and that made me think of the steaks old Jippy served there and I got hungry as hell. I figured to go there first and have a drink or two and a steak and get the lay of things.

"Just about then I run onto cattle bedded deep in sarvis brush—first one scared me, an old cow critter. I thought she was a bear, starting up there in the dark with a stomp and a snoof, but I was through the rest afore they could get out of bed, and by the faint light of the moon I knowed they was outlaws. I could see their white horns rise up around me all in a second, like them yucca flowers blooms on the desert.

"Once I come out onto a bench and over a dry meadow, and looked back and saw my dust a-risin' like smoke off'n that black mountain side.

"Then I run out of the timber into scrub cedars. A cloud come and covered the moon, so I couldn't see only the big things, and run old Tony right over them little trees and got my face slapped bad. Did you ever git a scrape from pine or cedar—oily trees? It's like somebody cut you open and poured in fire. But after a while we was down onto the desert, where there's nothing grows but lizards and shad scale, and there I could break old Tony into a lope. It was a mile to the crick bed, and I knowed that farms begun on the other side, and fences. I never reckoned on anything till I got there. But some son-of-a-bitch had run a drift fence right across that desert and Tony hit 'er at the end of his stride. It was like jumping in a net. I mounted the horn but grabbed leather with both fists and come down. Another horse but Tony would have cut himself in half, and if folks in that country built fences like they does out here, I guess even he'd o' done it, but this guy, this fence-builder—I'd say he come from Californy 'cept he didn't know how to build a fence—had just gone out there and put cedar posts in the desert about every hundred yards and hung some wire on 'em. I bet that wire had a give of ten yards. I could get enough slack to twist and break it with my hands. Then I lit a match to have a look at Tony and seen he was cut pretty bad on the chest, poor bastard. He wasn't in very good shape anyway after all summer on the mountain.

"But we was goin' to town, and by God we was a-goin'.

"So we went.

"Beyond the crick, farms come out and stopped the desert. From there on I knowed where the wire gates was in the fields. I could tell old man Stefans had put in alfalfa with water from his new well; that the widow James was pruning her apricots; that such and such a barking dog belonged to Hanky Hanks. Pretty quick I was out onto the Della road. Town was only half-a-mile. I could see the sign of the Hearty Laugh Saloon, but old Tony was a-commencin' to loosen behind, the way a pony does when he gives out. For a minute I thought I'd git off and walk him, and then I thought hell no, if I can't ride into town, I won't go at all; and I asked old Tony confidential if he thought he could make it, and he said he reckoned he could if I'd give him time, so we cut down to a walk and it was that way we hit Main Street.

"Bakers' Livery Stable happens to be first on your right. The place was all dark, but I knowed how to git in. I found some axle grease and doctored old Tony and give him a good feed, and then I went on to the saloon. But I took a detour on the way. I wanted to see my girl. It was only eight-fifteen, but maybe I could see her. So at the next street I turned off and went down to the café. I didn't go inside. The place was full and she was running up and down the tables. I waited there across the street where I could see it all—how she'd laugh and smile and make words with her mouth I couldn't hear to these folks she was a-waitin' on; and to me they was the luckiest people in the world. Oh, my, she was a sweet-lookin' maiden in them days! . . . Pretty face, pretty figure, her foot so light it never touched the ground. But when I seen her serve a plate, I knowed then why it was I'd come: I was sick of bein' laid agin the earth at night and bein' rubbed all day by rope and leather; I wanted them little hands to touch me. And then I looked at my own hands, covered with axle grease and blood, some Tony's, some of it mine, and I thought, 'You dirty hog, you ain't fit to mix with human kind; go git yourself respectable.' So I turned round and headed for the saloon.

"I can't say just how good that old saloon looked. Them swingin' doors was like the heavenly gates to me, 'cause I come a man a-wearied and blood was on me and my right leg burned like hell's own fire; but I had my own idees and I was on my way, and when you're that a-way, the rest don't matter.

"So I swung inside. There was Jippy at the counter rolling the boys for a drink; there was the green tables and the poker games; and I thought, 'Well, this is good; this is all right.' As I headed up to the bar, I seen an advertisement card saying Jean Harlow was a-gonna play next week in something, and I thought, 'By God, I'll do 'er again next Wednesday and take Maxine to see that.'

"Then I pounds a fist on the bar and calls for Jippy.

"'Hi, Powder Keg,' he says. 'With you in a minute,' and goes on rolling the bones.

"Well, after five minutes he come and I was mad.

"'What the hell, now,' I told him. 'Forgetting old friends?'

"'Naw,' he says, 'naw. . . .' And then, 'Been away?'

"I says, 'Gimme a double whisky.'

"When he come back, I told him to git me a steak rare—the best in the house.

"Then I had another whisky and commenced lookin' for society.

"A bunch of guys was standing there, so I goes over and asks 'em to have a drink with me; Jippy lined 'em up and we downed 'em and they kept saying 'okay' and 'swell,' so I had Jippy line 'em up again.

"Then these guys begun to talk, but not to me. They was working on a road some place that was cutting the Rocky Mountains in half, and all they could talk about was dough and WPA and CCC and Roosevelt, Roosevelt. I didn't want to hear about any of that, so I looked round again and seen old Hoopaloo over there at one of the card games.

"'Come out of that, you old bastard!' I told him, and he come. I set him up a drink and asked him first about Maxine. Yeah, she was fine. Yeah, prettier 'n ever. Nope, nobody had beat my time. She'd sure be glad to see me. . . . Been away?

"Well, I said, the hell with you; here's my steak and I'm hungry.

"So I swung round and begun to think better of old Jippy just because he'd brought me that steak.

" 'How's Hap?' I asks him.

" 'Dunno,' he says. 'Haven't seen him lately.'

" 'What happened about him and that Seamans girl? I heard her folks was goin' to court over it; or that's what a guy told me last week on the mountain.'

" 'Been on the mountain?' he says.

" 'Yeah, I've been on the mountain,' I says.

" 'Well, come to think of it,' he says, 'Hap *did* go out of town the other day . . . kind of in a hurry, too.'

" 'Was he ridin' a little cat-hipped sorrel?'

" 'Yeah,' says Jippy, 'believe he was. . . . Say, wasn't that *your* horse?'

" 'No,' I says. 'No. . . . Used to be, but I sold him to Hap.'

"The steak was getting cold right there under my eyes, but I don't know—I'd kindy lost my interest.

" 'Well,' I said, 'this looks like a good steak.' So I cut in, and do you know that steak was just a-turning, just a little bad, like milk, so that you can't decide whether to quit eating or go on. But I stayed with her—kindy felt I had to.

"I forgot to tell you—all this time somewhere in the back of the room or just outside, I couldn't say right where, they was a noise rising and falling and passing away, like the sound of the wind in them wires. I'd heard it but I'd been too much on the move to notice; and then it was I made my big mistake: workin' on that steak I had a chance't to think.

"What the hell was that sound? I stuck my head out the window, but there wasn't no wind. I come back and eat a while. Somebody put a nickle in the phony-graph and it played a song about 'I Surrender.' Then all of a sudden that wailing sound made itself into words, like the radio does when you tune her in square, and I heard it was a nagging woman. That's all it was—just a woman. I eat awhile and begun to get indigestion. She was after her old man for something back there behind the wall, poor devil. I feel sorrier for him than any man on earth and I never even *seen* him. While listening, I begun to feel the burning of my leg, my face, and a dozen other places I didn't know I had. I wearied fast, but that woman, she never wearied; she kept on forever like the wind does in them wires. I couldn't eat no more. Then the phony-graph song about 'I Surrender,' it run down-hill and quit, and everything in that room flattened out with it. I begun to think about my camp on Aspen Crick—just a little thought at first, but she got bigger mighty fast, like a train coming down a track, and then it seemed I wasn't a-getting enough air in that room; and how the others laughed and went on playing cards, right in the face of that woman there behind the wall, I couldn't see.

"I ordered me another double whisky; and when I'd drunk it, I went out of that place.

"I headed back up Main Street. When I come to the street of my girl's café, I kept a-goin', but once I looked. I seen the square of light the big window cut out of the sidewalk, and there come a sound of dishes, sudden-like, when somebody opened a door and went through into the kitchen, and that almost got me 'cause it meant Maxine. But I kept on. I was sour at the roots and couldn't change.

"I went and got Bill Baker out of bed and asked about my little cat-hipped horse, and he said Hap had it over to Joe Petrillo's, so I went and got out Joe, and he told me Jippy was right—Hap had rode him out of town, in a hurry. Then I was mad. I went back to the stable and give old Tony another pail of oats and a rub and told him we'd have to travel again; and he didn't care much for that, poor devil, 'cause he was a tired horse.

"As we shook out our bridle on the Della Road, day was trying to git over the mountain, but couldn't make it. Old mountain was too much for him, took up all the sky. . . . Kindy like Jacks in the doorway of the barn, only here I knowed what the mountain had to say 'cause up on Aspen Crick I'd heard him."

Dynamite finished his story. It wasn't like him, but he never asked me if I understood.

As we rode back over the knoll, they switched the

lights on in the mill, and I said, pointing, "It's lucky the power line crosses here or you might never have remembered that story."

"Oh, yes I would," he said. "I can't forget it. I'm married to that girl, Maxine."

NOBODY DANCED

JAYDEE had said he would get Dynamite. This happened Friday afternoon when dust from the big hammer mill settled in his brain and made it ache so badly that he left the feed-yard and drove home early to the village where he and Melanie, his young Arkansas woman, had recently set up housekeeping. California hadn't changed Jaydee Jones. He was six solid feet and two inches of Arkansas oak. He was strong—strong as any man in the county his size and weight, but not so strong as the dust hiding in the stems of hay. It made him sick first in his stomach and then in his head, and as he drove along he thought how good Melanie would look in the yellow pajamas he had bought for her birthday. He decided to take the next day off, because it was Saturday, and go with Melanie to the motorcycle races in Sacramento.

But when he got home, he couldn't find her. On the table in the front room—the house had two rooms, front and back—was a note somebody had writen: "You're a sweet one, you are. I'll meet ye sometimes else." Jaydee's head wasn't any too clear but he guessed this sentiment wasn't for him, and he recognized Dynamite's handwriting. When Melanie came home, they had hell about it.

Loyetta Mae, wife of Rollo Jane, the Okie, heard them from her trailer house parked in the vacant lot next door. She was getting supper for her husband, who drove a feed truck in the yards; and after Rollo and the babies had been fed and put away, she took a basket of laundry—the week's wash of Mrs. Jacks, the foreman's wife, in which were laid first the sheets because they were biggest and then the pillow slips and then the towels and last of all the news she had heard—and drove with it in her 1930 Chevrolet sedan back the two miles to the feed-yard.

Mrs. Jacks was a large woman who dressed extensively in beet-colored silk and managed her own affairs. She came onto the back porch herself in answer to Loyetta's knock, being concerned about seven linen doilies that had gone to the wash this week. She had taken in laundry herself at one time and knew how tempting linen doilies can be—even single ones.

Next morning Thelmo Jenkins, who does the cooking for Mrs. Jacks, went to the cookhouse to borrow an egg from old Mike, ranch cook, and when we came along at noon to eat our beans, all thirty of us knew Jaydee was going to get Dynamite before we had taken that second mouthful.

By three o'clock, everybody in the yards knew it. At the scale-house by the mill, where the boys sit for a smoke on the shady side while their loads are being weighed, Elmer said Jaydee would be with little Dynamite as the hammer mill with a bale of hay: "Grieves me—two men fighting over one woman."

Charlie Pell said particularly an Arkansas woman.

Jody said, "Her feet's itched her ever since Jaydee bought her them new shoes."

Cherokee said if Jaydee'd bought a wedding ring instead of shoes, it would have been a better thing.

So the talk went and the wind from the sea that blows always in this country carried off the words as it does pollen in the spring and spread them through the river hills, until even the remotest ranchers heard. At quitting time old Boyd Yarrow, who owns a wheat farm in the Happy Valley, stopped me at the barn and said he'd heard Dynamite had killed Jaydee Jones in a gunfight.

"Come to the opera house tonight," I said, "and see for yourself. Sid and Mary Koska are giving the dance."

They don't give operas in Bird Town any more. They've torn down the Palace Hotel and the gingerbread arcades and three of the saloons. But years ago before the railroads came, when the ground was young and an acre put up forty sacks of wheat, Bird Town was a great city. Every autumn grain ships gathered in the river from all the countries of the world and loaded the finest wheat America could give them; and up in Bird Town two miles away the opera girls played every night to a full house.

Now the girls and ships have gone, and the ground has gotten tired, and only Pete who runs the Last Saloon and Abe who runs the grocery can tell you of those busier days. Sid and Mary Koska came from Poland and bought the opera house for three hundred dollars cash and built a partition in the middle so they could live behind it and have their butcher shop in front. And it was here, on this particular Saturday night, that we were going to dance.

In the bunkhouse this made Cherokee get out his best choke-rag; and all through the river hills, in a dozen shanties built of gray-bleached boards, women were putting on those bright polka-dot dresses J. C. Penney sells at $4.98 and bundling up their babies and making sure the kerosene was out and the fire shut up well in the stove.

Bird Town after dark is the best lighted village in America. It is built at a crossroads where two power lines intersect, and the area of the city as measured by these intersecting lines is exactly seven poles. On each of them an electric bulb is fastened thirty feet from the ground, and these illuminate the seven shanties of the village—and their chicken coops and privies—in a strange way, much as descending flares might light a city ruined in war.

Also there is the Last Saloon, that for these forty years has kept its windows bright; and recently, to stay abreast of the times, Pete has added a new fangle: a red neon letter "X," which can be seen clear from the feed-yard and looks as though the devil himself had marked the place. Actually Pete is no devil. He is a sober man who never drinks himself and listens as patiently to our misfortunes as to the cold marsh wind that for these forty years has talked around the corners of the Last Saloon.

Tonight being Sid and Mary Koska's turn to give a party, their windows cut big yellow blocks from the board porch of the opera house and the dirt and gravel of the country road. Overhead the seven bulbs blazed on their poles, and altogether Bird Town looked as good to us as Broadway, New York City.

First, we heard Jaydee was over at the saloon, had been all day, and that he was beginning to boil. Some of us went over to see. Next, we heard Dynamite inside. It was his music that came out the open door. He played the French harp, the harmonica, and Elmer Lee played the fiddle. They were all the band we needed.

Mary Koska came onto the porch, tapping neatly with her little heels, and called to us, "Come along, boys, and grab yourself a girl." She looked very sweet and trim, standing there against the light with the side of her black head shining and her waist tucked in no bigger than a honeybee's, but the blood in us was cold and we said we'd be along directly, which meant we had to have a round of Pete's red-eye de luxe.

Ike carried the bottle. We gathered at the end of the porch and watched the people come. Ike said Jaydee's woman wouldn't have the gall to show herself.

"The hell she won't," said Jody. "Keepin' her out o' sight o' mankind is like keepin' bread from butter."

Cherokee said soberly, "Fellers, reckon there'll be a violence done this evening?" and he sounded like a little boy who's come to a baseball game and just can't wait for it to start.

People arrived, the women carrying the eats: the wrapped-up sandwiches and cookies that would make things easier on Mary Koska. Loyetta Mae led her batch of youngsters past us single file, like a mother duck, and at the tail came Rollo Jane all dressed to pieces and looking very poor. He switched off and came our way and took on a little reinforcement, but Loyetta never looked around. She was a good girl. Ever since '36 when the Oklahoma dust finished her and Rollo, she'd begun to drink a little herself—not much, just a nipper here and there during the day. They said she'd hit it up a little since the baby came. Living in a trailer does get a little slow.

Tex wandered in, long and brown, and Happy Stone and other folk that were Okies the same as Rollo and Loyetta Mae—Laplanders, to be more accurate. That is, they came from where Oklahoma laps over into the United States.

A Cadillac sedan pulled up along the porch, black and shiny as an undertaker's, and that was Jacks and his wife. She drove because it was her car. Jacks used the Company's when he traveled. He got out now, the rough old Arkansawyer, and looked about as comfortable in all that chromium and polish and in his best blue serge as a hickory tree would. Mrs. Jacks wore a hat that wadded up in layers like a honeycomb and carried a cake so big and white it shone clear through its wax paper, and made you swallow hard. Those angel-food cakes of Madam Jacks were heaven cut in ten slices.

At the door Jacks branched our way as Rollo Jane had done. Saturday night he was no boss. He could kick his heels once in the week and call the square dances and experiment with and explain his favorite subject, which was whisky.

When the bottle passed him, he opened his mouth wide with a sound like a locomotive letting off steam. "Boys, boys! . . . If I was you, I'd figure they was thousands and thousands of bottles of this here whisky but I had only one stomach."

"*Arch*-ibald!"

We saw something like a big boulder blocking up the lighted door.

"See you boys d'rectly," said Jacks. "There's my call to sassiety."

We watched him shuffle away and Cherokee said, "Poor old critter." Then the band hit up "Turkey in the Straw," and we sent the red-eye around again, faster, because our blood was feeling better, and decided it was time to go inside.

When we got there, we saw we'd overreached ourselves, that liquor'd fooled us like it has so many, because only Tex and Mary Koska were dancing. The rest of the party sat along the wall on benches all on the left-hand side of the room, Mrs. Jacks making a knot in the center with the other foremen's wives and everybody staring straight ahead and saying nothing. Really sociable, it looked. We turned right and lined up along that side of the room, wishing we were back outside. Sid Koska had taken away the meat from his showcase opposite the door and cleaned and swept the space in front of it, and the walls, too, but he couldn't very well paint them and the place looked pretty bare, pretty cold; and all those people never warmed it up a particle. The more they came, the colder it got. Some kids ran around hollering and cutting-up, and we watched them just as carefully as if they'd been the most important people in the world and the funniest. Whenever they acted smarty or tripped one another, we'd raise up such a squall as would make your hair stand.

Dynamite did his level best to put some limber in the air. Where the empty showcase met the wall he flamed in the corner. Right over him was a map of a beef steer showing all the proper cuts. On his left Elmer Lee crooked around a fiddle, causing the catgut to sing in pretty tolerable fashion. But Dynamite, he was made of music. He had a harmonica fastened to a barbed-wire holder, chuck wagon style, that kept it close against his mouth and left two hands free for the guitar. His dark red hair boiled up in curls; he wore a shirt the color of wine and his white hands flashed across it as they played the strings. He swayed and stamped and chewed that little harp as though it were an ear of corn, and music grew right out of him and filled the room.

But nobody danced—that was Dynamite's trouble.

When Jacks finally noticed us standing in some misery along the wall, he sang out: "Everybody dance!" That meant a Paul Jones and a chance to mix it up a little and warm the spirit. We spread around in a circle and when the band led away with "Red River Valley," we followed, weaving in the ladies'-chain from hand to hand. Slip-and-slide, it went, and slip-and-slide. If your feet are working, your face doesn't feel so bad. When the little ladies took our hand and smiled, we were ready.

"Dance with the gal *be*-fore you!" was the call; it paired me off against Maxine, Dynamite's wife. She gave me a dutiful smile because we were friends, and went on chewing gum. She looked like a fierce doll. For over a year now, ever since the baby came, she hadn't had the money for a permanent, and her black hair was running more to strings than braid. She'd made the brown dress she wore, and she was fiddling around behind it now, with one hand, at a green sash that had come undone. She had on brand-new slippers of the purple shade you see on certain kinds of lamps. They cost her $3.49 out of Monkey Ward's in Oakland. Or $2.49—she told me, but I forget. I tried to make her talk, but her eyes went away over my shoulder and found Dynamite, not proudly or very cheerfully—just because they had to.

Dynamite got the ladies' eyes; but when he got the rest of them, they worked. The hand I held in mine was hard as the sole of a shoe.

Maxine asked to be let go. Through all that racket she heard something I never did and hurried, wobbly on her high heels, to what used to be the coatroom of the opera house. In the old days, if you wanted to be swell, you could check your hat here as you came in. Tonight it was a nursery—no light, no furniture. Laid along the floor were bundles of that precious white-and-pink that couldn't be left at home, and I saw Maxine pick up one of them and hold it tight against her narrow chest as a child might cuddle a doll.

Melanie Jones came into the room just then. Without looking we all knew this. She wore a black dress that fitted to her small round body in a way that made your eye come back. Her breathing was deep and slow, as though maybe she had run a bit, and this flushed her oval face and barely parted her lips and made her pale eyes dance and sing; the whole picture was framed with little golden hair.

Mary Koska led her to a sink in the corner, behind the heavy wooden table where Sid does his butchering, and offered her a glass of beer, but Melanie didn't want beer.

"A whisky?" said Mary, sweetly, laying her hand on the girl's shoulder. "A little gin, dear?"

Melanie took a quick glass of gin and washed it down with water from the tap. Then Mary cracked open the door into the back of the house, and the two of them leaned through and drew faint cheers from the poker game. Ike and Jody, feeling their oats, waltzed up behind, pretending to be very smart, and caught each girl around the waist and swung her away laughing.

Over on the bench Mrs. Jacks and the foremen's wives tied their heads together.

Jacks took his coat off, stopped the music, and announced the time had come to square dance.

"Mother," he said to Mrs. Jacks, who still wore her hat, "take off that beehive and dance with your old man."

Mrs. Jacks wanted to look ladylike and severe, but couldn't manage it and blushed, exactly the way she used to in the sixth grade of the Hickory Bend Grammar School when Jacks carved her initials on his desk. But she would not dance, and she looked dark indeed when Jacks led Melanie Jones onto the floor.

Three couples joined him—Jody and Mary, and the Happy Stones, and Cherokee with Maxine.

"Oh, hold 'er tight," Jacks squealed. "Oh, hold 'er tight; Oh, *hold* 'er tight!"

The music broke full speed into "She'll be comin'

round the mountain when she comes, when she comes. She'll be drivin' six white horses when she comes," as though the band had suddenly boarded a train.

Feet began to polish the floor. Jacks squealed the way to go:

> "Left foot up
> And right foot down
> And meet yore honey
> Go round and round . . ."

Back and fourth that shuffling circle wove, broke, and built itself again.

> "Inside out
> And outside in
> And eight hands up
> And a-goin' agin."

The music poured along monotonous as running water and just as strong. It got inside those shuffling feet and told them where to go—Jacks could have saved his breath. It got inside all the dancers and led them as a stream does straws, slowly, quickly, gone suddenly from here to there. In the center of the room they made a weaving eddy. Maxine began to laugh. Her green sash came untied behind, but she didn't notice. When she finished "Chicken in the bread pan," Cherokee caught her by both hands and swung her off around the room and she flew in a brown whirl, laughing like a child pushed high on a swing.

Melanie floated on the face of the music. She fed herself upon it secretly, as a soft cloud builds in the sky. She didn't see her partner, Jody, or any of the people in that room, but only something far away that kept her lips parted just a little and brought a smile around the edges of her face—a funny kind of smile that wasn't there when you looked right at it.

I saw Dynamite watch her as he would a filly that he meant to break. We around the wall began to stamp and squeal. The poker game broke up behind the partition and gathered in the door, and most of their eyes were for Melanie. Youngsters who had been asleep woke up and cried, but nobody heard them. A very strange thing happened: that room itself began to change. Boards, windows, faces, silver hooks for meat behind the counter ran together in the music and seemed made of yellow light, and all of them went round and round with a stamp and a squeal and a stamp and a squeal. Only Melanie's pale eyes kept separate and looked far away.

When Jaydee came into the room, she simply closed them and went on dancing. We hushed our noise suddenly, but the music and the shuffle of the dance went on, and the room sounded like a train does when it enters a tunnel. Jaydee stopped inside the door and balanced back and forth, and you could hear him breathe. He was all flushed and spotted, and he looked mean—mean as a big dark tree that's going to fall on somebody. He stared and stared at Melanie as though he'd never seen her in his life before; and soon the music had him swaying in the proper time, but shakily, because he was drunk.

Jacks's face shriveled like a piece of ground in winter. Even the air was cold in that room, but he pretended not to notice and went on calling and calling until he sounded far away, like a man shouting in a valley. Melanie kept her eyes tight shut and Jaydee stared as if he'd made her open them.

Then a string of Dynamite's guitar broke with a "ping."

The party was over.

In one lurch Jaydee had crossed that floor. He kicked twice at the toe of Dynamite's boot.

"Are ye man enough?" he said.

Dynamite smiled. He didn't come to Jaydee's shoulder, but he laid down the guitar and it made the faintest musical echo.

Jacks said, "Boys, we're guests in this house."

Jaydee headed for the door, with Dynamite behind him, and I thought if he was Arkansas oak, then Dynamite was one of those cats that can live in a tree. He wouldn't fight only to hit, but with tooth and claw and anything that came in handy. He wore new spurs, I saw, that lifted brightly as he walked along.

They got to the open door and there a scream met them that was cold as murder.

"Bitch—dirty bitch!"

Outside in the ring of light beyond the porch Melanie

was flat on the edge of the road. Maxine stood over her holding a slipper—a purple slipper. She let Melanie get up on hands and knees and then knocked her down.

"Jesus Christ!" said Jaydee.

A spot was blossoming on Melanie's neck red as a bullet hole. She gathered suddenly and tried to tackle Maxine.

This time the slipper aimed for the tender piece of neck behind the head, the place a child can kill a steer, but Melanie came too fast and the sharp heel bit between her shoulder blades where the dress parted to show her soft back. She went skidding in the dust, both hands reaching for Maxine. They barely caught the hem of the brown dress and clung there for a long second that made your sweat come cold to see it, while the slipper rose and fell. She put her face up once and the slipper put it down; then with a quick jerk Maxine toppled.

The two of them rolled there in the dust like a couple of dogs.

Dynamite squeezed past Jaydee and jumped the steps; Jaydee followed but tripped over the rolling bodies and fell like one of those giants in a story book. Dynamite got Maxine by the arm. She bit the back of his hand and he let go and called her a bitch, holding his right hand with his left. Jaydee got a hammer-lock on Maxine from behind and tore her loose from Melanie and carried her screaming off beyond the rim of light. Melanie stayed down in the dirt, crying into it. Dynamite knelt over her, very white.

"Honey," he said, "don't cry."

She raised her face, stringy with hair, gashed all red by the slipper, and put it up against the cowboy's knee and cried and cried. He pulled a blue silk handkerchief from his hip pocket and tried to wipe away the blood, but it mixed with the tears and dust and made a dirty stain on the girl's face.

"Now you've got to get up," he said. "Come on, that's right."

He helped Melanie to stand and brushed off some of the dust. He wiped her face again and this time got it clean, although the blood came welling out again. He called to Mary Koska, "Mary, will you take her home?"

Off in the dark we could hear Maxine screaming, telling Jaydee about himself.

Mary came down the steps, and she took and comforted Melanie as if this was her own child; and Melanie, still crying, bent half-over, put her head deep in Mary's side, and cried and cried as she was led away.

Maxine never had stopped screaming, but she sounded muffled now, like a bad girl shut in a closet, and we knew Jaydee had locked her in a car somewhere.

When he came back inside the light, he was rubbing his face with both hands, as though maybe he would like to wash it, and then he saw Dynamite and snapped up straight. There he stood and there stood Dynamite with the yellow circle in between where the ripped-up ground was and a piece of Melanie's black dress. Their eyes met for a second; Cherokee on the porch coughed and it sounded like a gun going off; and then Dynamite started across the circle and Jaydee put his feet apart and watched him come.

Dynamite walked quickly, right up to Jaydee, and took him by the arm.

"How's your woman?" he said.

"Why—she's okay," Jaydee said. "She's—okay; how's your'n?"

"Same," said Dynamite. "What say we go over to Pete's and wash it down?"

"Sure," said Jaydee. "Yeah, that's a good idea."

They turned together, those two husbands, and started off across the road, and the seven lofty streetlights pinched their shadows down no bigger than two boys. Bird Town became silent all at once; Maxine had stopped her screaming. From behind us Jacks called out, "Everybody join hands; we got a dance here, don't forgit."

So we all went back inside and after a very little while, with only Elmer's fiddle, we made that old opera house shake and sing as it hadn't done since the grain ships lay in the river and the girls rolled long black stockings in what is now Mary Koska's pantry. Even Mrs. Jacks danced, with Jacks, which was the second most important thing to happen that evening.

DYNAMITE'S DAY OFF

Dynamite had asked for Sunday off to go to the rodeo at Sacramento and had been refused, and his wrath was greater than Achilles'. He had entered the bronc riding and steer decorating and hoped, for one afternoon, to forget he was married to a wife and four children and worked for three dollars a day, seven days a week, in a feed-yard full of silly fat cattle. Instead he and I drove two cars of steers to the station, and I saw a spark kindling in his eyes, that threatened to explode all twenty-six years of his Utah brimstone and powder.

We put the steers in the loading corrals and got ready the first of two empty cattle cars that stood on the siding. Its door stuck, as car doors always do; and Dynamite, in wrenching at it, crushed his hand against the side of the car and drew it out bleeding, with an oath. The bit of animal yellow in his blue eyes widened. He unfastened the bull-board and dropped the wooden apron, and I pulled forward the sliding wings of the chute. We walked down the cleated ramp to where the steers stood in the crowding pen, staring at us like great fat dogs. We wanted twenty-seven in each car—one for Los Angeles, one for Denver. Dynamite counted them by. We crammed the twenty-seven in the car with terrible shouts. We climbed over the gray bleached fence and cut loose the car. I took the Johnson bar, which is a kind of pry that fits under the wheels and will move a train if your back is strong enough, and Dynamite pushed, and we got her rolling.

When the second car was in place and ready to load, we went down into the crowding pen and I counted the steers by. There were twenty-eight.

I said to Dynamite, "They're only twenty-six steers in that first car.

He ran up quickly—he hadn't yet said a word to me—and counted my cattle again through the slats of the car. There were twenty-eight. Then he began to swear. Once in a small California town I saw a Filipino run amuck and come screaming down Main Street, flailing with a chain at everything in his way. That was how Dynamite sounded. His voice rose into a wail, sing-song, like a maniac's: "God damn, God damn, *God* damn . . ." He swung ape-fashion inside the car, hanging from the overhead beam, and kicked a big red steer in the face until its nose bled and it backed out into the ramp. I dropped the bull-board and held the rest.

We got the Johnson bar again and went to work; and by the time we had the first car back in place, we felt as though we had moved the whole Southern Pacific.

Then Dynamite went for the steer. Now when an animal has once been loaded and come out, to get him back again is like getting a convict back to jail. Dynamite and that steer went round and round. The steer got mad. Dynamite got madder. The steer ran him up the fence. Dynamite got a post and hit the steer over the head till one eye was shut and the blood ran from its nose, and he kept on till the animal gave a shake of its head and a bloody snort and ran up into the car.

"Well," I said, "it's a good thing they don't eat the head."

"The son-of-a-bitch," said Dynamite.

Our horses were tied at the far end of the corrals. As we got on, I saw a black pick-up truck drive alongside our cars of cattle and stop.

"There's the boss come to give you hell," I said.

We led the horses through a side gate and around toward the tracks. I saw somebody that wasn't the boss at all get out of the pick-up, standing on one leg, and draw a crutch after him.

"It's that old man," said Dynamite, not to me, but to the earth in general, as you would say a profane thing. From him this was profanity. He and old Reuben

Child were great friends. Dynamite could admire any man who was a Texan and who, besides, had been a champion roper and rider. Rube lived now in a house the Company had given him, and like an old hunting dog never failed to know when cattle were on the move and hurry down in his pick-up to be there.

He waved the crutch at us and took a shovel from the bed of the truck with his other hand. He had backed his pick-up to the low ridge of sand that collects along the tracks in front of the chute—bedding from the cars, kicked out by the cattle.

I got off and tied my pony and said, "Hey now, old man, stealing our sand?"

"Oh, no," said Rube, "the Company told me I could have it," and his face lit up as though they had given him a new house.

"You'd better hand me that shovel," I said.

I thought Dynamite had ridden on. I knew he was ready for one of his evenings at the village saloon with Pete, the bartender, the trustee of our misfortunes. I rather wished he had gone on, but he couldn't—he couldn't quite pass up old Rube. He got off sulkily and came to us.

"Hello, Dynamite," said Rube, raising his Texan's drawl till he sounded like a little girl.

"Hi, Rube," said Dynamite.

"Come on," I said, "there's another shovel in the truck. Get busy."

In five minutes we had the pick-up loaded.

"That's enough fellers," said Rube. "I only want it for the dooryard. Here . . ." he said, reaching into the compartment of the front seat, "here, this is Sunday. Have a drink on it."

"Naw," said Dynamite, "I gotta go."

"Have a drink," said Rube.

"I gotta be going." Dynamite untied his brown nag from the fence.

"Come on, have a drink," said Rube and held out the bottle.

Dynamite took it, holding the tie-rope with his other hand, and tilted down a good long shot. "That whisky's all right," he said.

The bottle went around and Rube gave it back to Dynamite for another shot. "Say," said Rube, "isn't that saddle a Harney Lee?"

"Yeah," Dynamite said, "one the Evans Company named after him."

The saddle was older than Dynamite himself. The cover had peeled from the high flat horn and worn clear away from places on the stirrup leathers, so that you could see the latigo straps; its skirt had shriveled like the skin of a drying fruit, but in the center of the tree, where a man did his riding, the leather had the color of dark mahogany shining in the sun—a deep red quality—and here was all the life of the saddle.

The wind blew the mane of the brown nag and made him put his ears up, so that he and the saddle were a picture for a book.

Dynamite looked at them proudly. "That's a hell of a fine saddle, Rube," he said.

Rube sat down on the runningboard of the car, facing west, with the sun full on him, took a sack of Bull Durham from his pocket, and began to roll a cigarette. The wind bent the brim of his cattleman's hat and slapped him in the face, but he pushed the hat back with one hand and went on rolling the tobacco in his other, and never lost a grain.

"Shore is a country to blow," he said.

Rube was a veteran of the range. His face, drawn by years of pain from the broken hip, had on it the indelible stain of western sun. His large clear eyes seemed always to be searching some horizon; his ears were classic American, protruding just a little; and there was about him a peculiar decency and patience. When he smiled, his face shone almost in a heavenly way, as Lincoln's did.

"You fellers ever hear the story of Harney Lee?"

"I never did," said Dynamite.

Rube held the cigarette up to his mouth and licked the end of it affectionately. We knelt beside him, close to the track, and the cattle in the car above us stomped around and kicked out little puffs of sand through the slats of the car. Rube smiled.

"Makes me laugh to see cattle nowadays. Gracious, they ain't cattle; they's responsibility. Gotta be fed this, gotta be fed that, gotta be fed this very time o' day. Why, where would them great outfits of old time have been—

Turkey Track and Circle Dot—if they'd had to go out every day at half-past two and *feed* their cattle? Those fellers depended on their cattle, not their cattle on them. And by cattle I mean longhorns. It was them built the West and don't you never forget it." Rube stuck the cigarette in his mouth, but it was not right and he spat it out and threw it away. "My story is about the time when cattle still had horns . . . about the greatest rider that ever rode and the wind that made him great and the horse that killed him.

"In the fall of '98 we was coming from Chihuahua toward the Rio Grande and, fellers, that's a long country—long and dry—and when ye've been out sixteen weeks, she's up hill all the way. We counted two hundred horses and six thousand longhorn steers. Red Handle was our boss—finest ever that trailed a herd—and his top rider was Harney Lee. I think there was thirty-three of us all told. Men was cheap in them days; it was cattle cost the money."

Dynamite interrupted, "This here Harney Lee—what did he look like?"

"Oh, he was a Texas man," said Rube. "Looked like a giant but he weren't so big. Had a mustache . . . eyes that got narrer at the outside. You can see his picture in books. . . . We'd been out all summer with the wagon and was headed home with what we'd done, six thousand old mosshorns from 'way back that till we come along had never seen a horse from the day they was born. Some had the Hour-glass and Horseshoe brands; some was mavericks virgin pure. What I mean they was cattle! You got up on a high place and give a squall or two and all over the county puffs of dust went up and that meant cattle heading for the next state. But we rode with 'em step for step, and by the time we started for the Rio Grande, they knowed a cowboy.

"One afternoon I seen 'em acting queer. Five or six would stop together and raise their heads and sniff and stand a while; and in a herd the better part of four mile long this slows you up considerable. Well, I was a youngster then and when I got in for supper, I asked Red Handle what was the matter—he was eatin' beans; never eat nothing but beans, old Red, but he sure was a boss. He could water six thousand head in a hole the size of this room and never get it muddy. . . . 'Dust,' he says. 'They smell a dust somewhere's,' and went on eatin' his beans.

"Well, that put a wiggle in my spine, but I never said so. I noticed the wind had come up a little, and when the cocktail riders got in and the night-hawkers was ready to start, I saw Red go over and talk a while to 'em. There begun to be something in the air. Cookie gathered in his washing and his pots and pans like he'd seen the enemy already. At daylight we was on the move. We kept the trail three hours, but that daylight never growed. Then we knew it was dust. By noon she'd rose up there in the north big and blue, like night had got around that way and was coming down on us;

and when she got closer, she turned red around the edges as if fire was in her, and then yellow. We went slower and slower. By now, them steers would stop every few feet and snort and sniff the air, and when two o'clock come they wasn't moving at all. We'd had 'em to water at a dry lake on a piece of country flat as your hand, and it was plain they'd go no farther. Pretty quick them as had laid down got up. It become terrible dark. Then altogether them cattle begun to move—*south.* They was like water after a rain, altogether, a-walkin' just as steady, and when the first grains of sand hit 'em, they begun to trot, all six thousand. Then we rode.

"Ever been in dust? Well, when you have, don't never worry no more 'bout going to hell 'cause you've been there already. In a duster you burn just as slow. It's like the devil come at you first with sandpaper, then with fire, and oh-mercy-me, how he does hurt! Seems he's gonna skin the clothes right off you and eat out your eyes and nose and ears like fire eats out a holler tree. You see him hit them mesquite bushes—big spiny fellers thirty feet across—and shrink 'em till they're no bigger'n a porcupine. Behind every bush and rock he makes an eddy, as does a running stream, but don't git in there or you *will* choke, 'cause there the sand boils right straight up. You'll smell the stink o' creosote bushes being broke and chewed up; you'll see chuck-wallas, and such, run under foot till you think your pony'll trip hisself—they can't find no hole the dust don't smoke 'em out of. And maybe you'll look around all of a sudden and find cattle on both sides, and then you won't know what to do, so you drift with 'em. Don't never try to head a herd; it can't be done. Sometimes you can bend 'em, but head 'em—never. If you meet a rider, you think it's Billy-the-Kid out to rob a stage—face in a bandana, hat tied hard and fast, but some way the rheumatics has took him and he's bunched like an ape in the saddle. One feller I saw lose his hat, and that's just barin' your head for the execution. What I mean it's a serious thing. He had a gunny sack tied behind his saddle, but before he could get to it, I seen a blush start up his face that meant the skin was going.

"Once I looked around and *did* see only cattle on both sides and there was nothing I could do. I thought left was out and bore that way, edging mighty easy through them horns, and finally I run clear of cattle and found two other fellers and knowed then that I had the flank. We drifted quite a while, shaping the herd the best we could, feeling them steers more 'n we saw 'em, and after a long time Harney Lee come up behind us with five men. He'd been clear around the tail of that herd. Red Handle'd sent him with half the riders they could find and kept the other half, and now we was organized. Six of us strung along the flank and three went up with Harney on the point. He rode a little Steeldust horse, I remember—one of them Texas ponies just the color of dust, and it was hard to follow him. We stayed all day, bending the cattle as we could, and that wasn't much 'cause cattle traveling that way don't have much give in 'em. Pretty quick it got dark. This here was night, gen-u-ine. Once the dust blew clean away over us like a rainstorm does and we could see a piece of the moon up there, brown and rotten as an apple. Then the dust come on again, and all night it kept after us and all next day, and it seemed we was a-goin' backward where we'd been last summer. . . . I mean the year itself was goin' back. We'd pass a gully or a rock we knowed, and they'd rise up there to say we'd wasted our time and never would get home.

"That day four more fellers joined us, but we didn't eat and seen no sign of the *remuda*. I never cared; I had my best horse under me—a buckskin bronc named Anesthetic, and what I mean he'd put many a man to sleep. But when that kind tries you and sees you don't fade, they become good horsey. For a tough ride give me a buckskin every time; they can't be beat.

"Well, the second day got on . . . we couldn't tell the time—it all run together and become evening. And now the steers was dryin' up and gettin' mad; sal-*i*-ver hung outer their mouths like spiders was inside a-spinnin' threads and you had to be chary 'bout getting close, or them big leaders would turn and root you one. But they kept right on; they was walkin'-mad.

"Harney would look 'em over and ride up and down the line. We got to calling him general and saluted as he come, and other things men does when they're very tired. He was so all-over-dust you couldn't tell who it was coming 'cept by how he set his horse, always for'rd thataway in the saddle, ready to make his ride. He'd laugh at us, blowing dust off his mustache, and call us chuckwallas-sons-of-bitches. He told me one thing: to keep my forty-five inside my pants or the sand would ruin it. He packed two guns hisself. I could see 'em bulge under his chaps; and he rode a low-lyin', double-rigged saddle with the short cantle and high horn—one they named after him.

"Oh, he was a giant of a man, Harney Lee, but to look at he weren't so big. . . .

"Now after quite a spell—might have been noon, might have been three o'clock—he comes to me and says, 'Young Rube, we're a-gonna bend this herd. I want you to ride and tell Red Handle I need men.' Reckon my face showed what I felt—that bending the herd would be as easy as bending the storm—'cause he sobered clear up and says, 'We got a alkali lake ahead of us and the water's poison; we can't let the cattle to it.' Well, then I rode. I got lost. I dried clear out. I couldn't find the end of the herd. Once I passed an *ocatilla*, a cactus that's all joints and fingers, and that's the only time I ever wanted to be a cactus, 'cause them *ocatillas* can breathe through their stems. Then I found Red and he looked awful poor; he'd had a fall and sprained his arm. He took eight fellers and told 'em what Harney wanted and all he said was, 'All right, boys. I want to hear ye've made this ride.'

"I led the way back and when we come again upon

the left flank the sky got terrible dark and then all of a sudden she lighted up and there was the greatest sight on which *my* eyes ever laid. There was Harney Lee and seven men goin' alone agin the point, *and they had her bent!* Seven of 'em had her bent. They rode her down out of a per-pet-tual circle, riding close together, single file, with not enough room between for cattle to come through, and always the tighest part of that circle was again the herd, and here the guns was flashing and the boys would make their ride—pressing in and in; and now a big steer would take to 'em and run 'em out of line, and they'd shy off and come round the loop and hit the herd again; and always Harney led 'em, pouring fire in the air from both his guns. We hurried and joined up with 'em and made a bigger, heavier circle, with never room between us for a steer to pass; and we bent them critters clear around.

"Them as was fightin' mad and wouldn't bend we shot, and the rest kept on—but always to the right, just a little to the right. We hit a kind of water course that in such country was like a line on the palm of your hand, but it helped; and here we done what no men ever done—we milled that herd. Yep, milled her. Red shaped her from the other side but Harney Lee it was that milled her, tucked her in till she was running like a rattler on her own tail. Time and time again he led us in, flyin' in the twilight like a man who rode the wind. . . . Slowly she wound up and run down, and some critters at the inside fell and was chewed like meat in a grinder; and then just as we thought we had 'er, the whole thing come undone, snapped open like a willer branch that's been rolled up, and away went them critters down the plain. Three times we rolled 'em up and three times they come undone, but on the fourth they stayed. . . .

"I never seen such a cattle to run; but they was plumb tuckered now and we backed off some and give 'em slack. You could see them steers was done—down by the head and down by the tail, and for old-time cattle that's a precious rare sight. As we left 'em to git reconciled, the storm quit altogether and there was the sun goin' down over there behind some hills.

"We held the herd all night and next morning the day broke clear and we eased 'em up this wash into a new country. By noon we'd found water, running water, and made camp. Toward evening here come Cookie and the *remuda*, two hundred ponies. They'd drifted with the storm the same as we. The wranglers said they'd gone ahead and the herd had followed 'em like ponies will a man in the dark—in a way, that's the rest of my story, but anyhow . . . from this stream of running water Red got the idea for going home along the Coche Hills where there was more streams like it and a storm couldn't git right to us if it come again. We laid over a couple of days and within three more we'd hit a rim-rock country with canyons and some timber.

"We all stood turns night-hawking the ponies, three

of us, usually, 'cause there was Mexicans around and this far from home we couldn't take no chances. There's nobody loves good horseflesh as does a Mexican.

"This particular night Harney Lee was on the graveyard shift, him and a couple of fellers—one called Sleepy Head and another silly kind of feller called Jack. The herd was on a slope above a canyon, and when the next shift come, it got to Jack first. He'd seen old Sleepy dozin' over there and had an *i*-dee for some fun. He gives his horse to the others to hold and slips over there right easy with his quirt behind old Sleepy.

"You know how horses are at night, up and down three or four times, and so long as some are up and feedin' the rest won't scare, but this particular night it happened all the herd was asleep, and when Jack smacked old Sleepy's nag across the rump he jumped twenty feet down hill and bucked old Sleepy off and broke in two and went down through that herd just a-buckin' and a-raisin' hell; and them ponies was to their feet like one horse and away down the canyon. . . . Well, square in their way was Harney Lee. You boys never seen horses comin' at you wild in the dark but it's a terrible thing. They'll run you down the same as steers and twice as quick. Their shoes knockin' the stones sends out all manner of sparks—red and yeller and blue. Harney seen it comin' and could have got away, but instead he turned his pony and begun to ride—same little Texas pony he'd rode through all the dust. He knowed how horses will foller a man by night if you give 'em just the right amount of room, and he figured to wind 'em up somewheres and lead 'em home. And that's what he did. We found the herd next day up again the rim-rock, and in the canyon by the trail lay Harney where he'd fell. . . . A badger'd dug his hole right there." Old Rube stopped talking. The cold spring wind slapped through our clothes and made the wiry grasses sing in the ditch beside the track. "Pity," said Rube. . . . "Pity he couldn't have died upon his greatest day; but all of us can't do that—we gotta die in beds or, if we're lucky, just a-doin' our job like Harney done."

Dynamite gave a wet sniff and tried to hide it in a sneeze, wiping his mouth with his shirt sleeve. There was a single poppy growing in the track between two ties and he plucked it and mashed the petals through his fingers. "Well, by God, Rube," he said, "that was a good story."

THE WIND OF PELICAN ISLAND

FROM outside the bunkhouse, far into the night, we heard a sound as though a kettle were boiling on some distant fire.

"Don't care much for that sound," old Rube said. "That's the kind of wind talks to cattle."

We edged our boxes nearer the wood stove and Dynamite said to Rollo Jane, "Rollo, tear up that box and throw it in the fire; you Okies is used to sitting on the floor."

Rube continued, "Like I told T. S. Ordway this morning 'bout them Mexican steers you fellers drove. 'T.S.,' I says, 'you got the biggest feed-yard in the West; you been feeding Herefords and Durhams for years, but these here just ain't feed-lot cattle. How do you know they'll eat? How do you know what ailments they'll take? These cattle is from the old longhorn strain and you can't predict 'em.' 'Well, Rube,' he says—you know how slow he goes when he's thinkin' a lot—'Well, Rube,' he says, standing there all duded up in felt and tweeds, 'maybe they oughta go on pasture first till we see how they gets along.' And that's how come him to call the barges and you fellers to be over here on Pelican Island."

I said, "Thanks, Rube," and shivered.

The bare boards of the bunkhouse didn't begin to stop that wind. They simply focussed it along their cracks until it struck us like a beam of ice. The kerosene lantern smoked and flared and ran a dirty shadow on the wall; the wind rustled old copies of the San Francisco *Examiner* on a table by the window, and brought us the damp decaying odor of the delta island.

"Rollo," said Dynamite, "did ye hear me speakin' to ye a while ago?"

He and Rollo were friends, though Rollo had been a dirt-farmer and drove a tractor in the yards at $3.65 a day, and helped us only when we had a lot of cattle to move. Next him by the stove sat Sims, the perfectionist, the artist on horseback. He rode his saddle like a bronze statue. Then came Reuben Child, the old Texan longhorn who had been one of Ordway's cow-foremen till he fell from a truck and broke his hip. Now he said, "You fellers is too green to be this far from timber. If you want wood on Pelican Island, dig a shovel-full of ground."

"Hear that, Rollo?" said Dynamite.

"Shore 'nuff," said Rollo mildly and never moved.

Dynamite rose and went outside, letting in a swirl of wind that sent doors slamming through the house and nearly ruined the lamp. Again we heard the faraway sound, a tiny shrill note, as though a mosquito were angry or a fly had gotten caught somewhere in a spider's web.

"Don't care much for that sound," said Rube.

Dynamite came back with both hands full of dark brown earth, kicked open the stove, and dropped in the dirt. He turned the damper till the flames roared up the black pipe. "Now damn you, you wise old man," he said to Rube, "if this don't burn, we'll take that crutch of yours and it will!"

"Smell it?" said Rube.

A smell like that of greasy leaves burning on damp ground filled the room.

"Whew," said Dynamite, "smells to me like somebody needs a bath."

Rollo Jane looked into the stove and said, letting his voice fade away like a little child's and die, "She's just a-burnin'. . . ."

Sims said, "What a hell-of-a-way to spend Saturday night, watchin' the ground burn." He reminded us we were spending this night away from home on a windy island in a marsh with a cold supper inside us, and why we were. He said again, "Wait'll Ordway hears his ground will burn. He'll have a way to make money on it."

T. S. Ordway had bought thirty-nine cars of Mexican steers. When we trailed them from the station to the feed-yards, he stood by the door of his big Lincoln sedan and never said a word. T. S. Ordway lived in that car. His office was the back seat. In it he drove thousands of miles each month between his various ranches, banks, and office buildings that were as common through the West as sagebrush and dry river beds. Men said of him that if Western Union had an office in the town, T. S. Ordway had one. But he was his own main office. He did the business himself; and when he got out and stood beside the car, with the hair turning a little wispy under his city hat and the skin loosening from his rock-bound jaw, he was still all man—all the way up. He watched us pass without a word and before half the cattle had gone by, got back into the car and told the chauffeur to drive away.

We put the steers on barges and ran them down the slough into the river and up another slough to Pelican Island. When we trailed them down the levee road, Dynamite and I were in the lead and the cattle followed, as orderly as soldiers. Modern stock would have been all over the place, but these old critters just put their heads into our ponies' tails and trudged along.

They made a queer sight—all sizes, shapes, and colors, but most of them were pintos, black and white, and there were also many solid blacks, descendants of the vicious Spanish cattle that once ran along the Rio Grande. For shipping, they had been dehorned six inches from the head: only the stumps were left, big around as your wrist, but you could imagine what those horns had been.

We had trouble on Little Betty slough that crosses the Island as a kind of outlying defense against the marsh. On one side is a field of young grain; on the other, a wilderness of reeds and ponds—a foreign land lying beyond water. Here, no matter what the season, it is always earliest spring. The wiry grasses, the clumps of low growth that look risen from the bottom of the sea, have in them every color of green. Kildees run crying over the mud flats; ducks go silently in squadrons down the sky. Everywhere there is an almost inaudible squashy noise, as of someone walking on a damp lawn. Every sound is in a minor key and no color is quite true, but shades into some other, suggesting, promising. This is the unknown land where life moves in water as at its beginning, and overhead the north wind blows and makes the grass stems sing like wires and brings small clouds upon the sky that lie close together and overlap, like feathers on the breast of a bird.

The marsh is a strange thing, but it was the field of grain that gave us trouble. A drainage ditch six feet wide and seven deep separated it from the road and was full of water; hungry steers trying to cross fell in and swam along until we snagged them with our loops and dragged them out. My pony, Old Barb, and I had a bad time with a big yellow steer. We played him like a giant trout to a low place in the bank and then, when I turned Old

Barb sharply away and stung him to make him hit that line, a horn stuck in the bank and Barb hit the end of that rope and went straight in the air, like a dog at the end of a chain, and came back over. I felt him coming and got away in time. We rose together, sticky with mud, and he looked at me as if to say, 'You got us into that.' But on the next try we snaked out our fish. We had to do this several times before we reached the pasture that covers all the western part of the Island. There is good feed on it and a nasty bog called "King Tule" on the west side toward the bay, but ordinarily cattle won't go there; and if Rube hadn't talked to old T.S. about these Mexicans being so unpredictable, we could have come home and had our Saturday night. As it was we went to the bunkhouse of the farm crew, and the only good thing we found there was Rube himself, who had followed us in his pick-up truck like an old dog on the scent. Every one else had gone. So we rustled around and found some cold stew and built a fire afterwards in the drafty old bunkhouse, and settled down to talk ourselves into a better mood.

And now Sims had spoiled it. Sims was a kind of sour apple anyway. He said, "Nowadays it takes money to make money. If I had what Ordway got, *I'd* go to El Paso and buy *me* thirty-nine cars of steers at six cents a pound; and I'd lay 'em in here at seven, hold 'em four months, and let 'em go to the butchers at ten. That's business."

"Sure," said Dynamite, "good enough business for me."

Rube said, "Remember this—it takes a big man to make big money. Didn't T.S. build this feed-yard himself out of a marsh? Didn't he build the levees and turn the mud flats into gold? Likely he will clean up on these Mexican steers, but think of the risk he takes. What did he pay for 'em? . . . Sixty thousand dollars. Stands to lose it, don't he? What if they takes sick, or the market drops, or the butchers don't like 'em? Where is he then? I tell you it needs a big man to make big money."

"Goddamn," said Dynamite. "I wish't I'd grow a little."

"I'll tell you a story," said Rube, "about T. S. Ordway that'll show you what I mean. Many years ago when he was starting out in life he took a contract as builder on a dam, a sub-contract it was, and under it he went out and bought materials and hired men. He did the job all right, finished on time; but when he came for his money, they gave him script instead. He never said a word. He went to town that night—Las Vegas, I think it was—and sat down to a poker game. Now up till then he'd never played a game of cards for money, but he sat down *that* night to play for money; and in the morning he got up with cash enough to pay his men. He said, 'I never paid my men in script and I never will.' . . .

"Now that's what T. S. Ordway done in Las Vegas," said Rube, and pulled a sack of Bull Durham from his shirt pocket and began rolling a cigarette. The wind rattled the shingles on the roof, and made a thousand sighing and complaining sounds, with always at the back of them that little note, higher now and sharper, like a wasp getting ready to sting.

"Don't care at all for that sound," said Rube. "Ever see wind talkin' to cattle?"

Sims said, "If you mean those Mexicans we drove today, they're too poor to listen."

"They're longhorns," said Rube. "I seen their daddies in Chihuahua when the wind come whisperin' of dust. Then they traveled."

Rollo Jane, who until now had spoken hardly a word, became excited at this mention of the wind and said, "It was wind done for me. Three year in a row it come, bringin' the dust. We'd get the land all worked up nice, put in the seed, and watch her come; and every year when she got about so high"—he made a measurement between two fingers—"the dust took her . . . buried her there in the fields. We prayed for rain but that feller up there sent us the dust instead."

Sims spoke now: "Like back home, when the apples get about so big"—and he made a measurement between *his* two fingers—"the cyclones come."

Dynamite opened the stove and the wind blew out a little puff of ashes. "Fire's dead."

Rube stretched and yawned. "Look outside, young feller. There's a whole island to burn."

Dynamite drew back his hand in a mock gesture of menace, but went outside.

"Minds me of one time years ago," said Rube, "a young feller from Stockton—I forget his name—went out at night to look for cattle on Rainbow Island over there; but he never come home. Next day they tracked him to the edge of a peat burn, and that was all they could do."

"Oh, these islands will burn," said Sims.

"Take Pelican, here," said Rube. "One place over in the pasture burned thirteen year till old T.S. come along with his pumps and flooded the land."

Dynamite returned carrying a small box with dirt for the fire, letting in a hostile blast of air that took the papers off the table and drew dust right out of the floor.

"See them steers?" Rube asked, and then he said, "Mercy, goodness . . . I plumb forgot to milk old Daisy Bell—sittin' here gassin' with you fellers; and she and her baby out in the cold wind. You're no good!" He dismissed us with a wave of his crutch and stumped away into the night. We heard the sound of his pick-up start and die out down the levee. It left us very much alone.

For a while we sat around the stove listening to the wind whine and groan and pick away at the old bunk-house. A board got loose somewhere and went to slamming; and always up high was that wasp, sharpening himself, getting closer and closer.

Dynamite went outside, came back, and said to Sims, "Lookie here." His eyes had become extra blue, I saw, so I went outside, too.

We stood on the porch and the wind whipped us with the moist, rotting odor of the marsh. We could see the levee clear to the landing, and everything was all right down there. Off the other way—west toward the bay where clouds running low under the moon made the fields go light and dark—we could see the silver grain, and beyond it in the pasture something was wrong. The steers hadn't lain down; they weren't feeding the way hungry cattle should. They stood together in groups of four or five, or maybe ten or twenty—you couldn't tell, they were so far away; but when the moonlight came just so, you could see their heads go up and a flicker of it running on their stubs of horns.

Dynamite said, "I don't like the look o' them steers."

Sims said, "Aw, what could be the matter with 'em?"

Rollo came out and joined us.

"Think I'll take a ride down there," said Dynamite, and went across the yard toward the barn, braced forward into the wind. I followed him and so did Rollo, and before we had our horses curried off, Sims came and began saddling his Appaloosa mare. I could tell he was mad.

When he got outside, he set the mare up and spun her like a top, as though they were in Madison Square Garden.

Dynamite, standing doing up his tie-rope, never looked around. He said to me, patting the rump of his brown nag, "This horse's got a lot of Steeldust in him." The horse had no more Steeldust in him than I had, but

Dynamite liked to think so, because that was the breed of Texas ponies. Rollo opened the barn door wide to bring out his black Percheron, and the wind sucked in behind him and swept the floor clean all in one "whoosh." He clambered up the great beast, who was just as slow and gentle as Rollo, and we started.

The wind flattened the clothes against our backs and blew the ponies' tails out all around them like the skirts of women. It pushed the clouds away from under the moon and made our shadows run before us, cut so clear that when they crossed a ditch or board, we wanted to duck our heads. It cried and laughed and died beside us in the reeds like a complaining child, and then it would come again with a rush and a sweeping of a thousand wings, and you could hear that little note away up there, that wasp getting readier and readier.

"See what I see?" said Dynamite.

I could see cattle standing up. All over the pasture they rose, stretched, and stood together facing us, sniffing the wind.

"Well, we're here," I said, and as if they heard me speak, that field of steers turned all together and began to move. Slowly and surely they followed down the wind toward the great bog of King Tule and Oyster Neck, that juts out sharply in the bay, and they never made a sound.

"Take your good holt," said Dynamite, "'cause now we're gonna ride."

He leaned from his saddle and flung open a wire gate,

and it was my bad luck to stay and shut it. The others went away down the field like bits of darkness blown by the wind. There was no question what to do; we had to get around the herd and beat those cattle to King Tule, and we had to do it quick. I got aboard Old Barb and set sail. The steers were walking quietly. I passed close to them; they paid no attention. I thought, "This is absurd. This isn't a stampede. These are gentle cattle walking over a pasture."

First, I overtook Rollo who sat his Percheron like a sack of meal, drumming with both heels and swearing helplessly to see me pass; and then I got close to Sims and saw him holding in his mare, afraid of that bad ground. Barb passed him going like Man o' War for the wire, and I felt proud. Dynamite was far ahead. How he got speed out of that brown nag was the mystery of all the world of running horses, but he got it—plenty of it. He already had turned past King Tule and flanked the herd.

A cloud covered the moon, and in that darkness the wind made up its mind to do us no good. It rose and sounded through the wiry grasses and brought that wasp down out the sky and set him right behind us. The cattle broke into a trot. They weren't excited; they were like old men going home, and a thought of Mexican deserts ran across my mind, shrouded in dust, with cattle moving shadowy as ghosts. Barb went for a *matrero*, which is what the Mexicans call a cunning steer, and sent him back toward firmer ground. They would go when you pushed them, but you had to push them, every one. A big dun three-year-old had his eye on the reeds of King Tule, a hundred yards away. Twice Barb scooped him up and put him where he belonged, but on the third run the steer dodged, Barb spun in the mud, and I heard an awful sound—a sound like somebody had taken a stick and wrapped it in a towel and broken it over his knee. And as I heard it, Barb went away under me and I floated in air. It was a leisurely thing. I thought, "Good, I'm clear of him. This isn't bad. Now I'm going to hit on the back of my shoulder." And then I hit.

I wasn't hurt; I didn't even lose my hat. I got up right away and saw the steer wave his tail and head for the King Tule, and then I saw Rollo bear down like a locomotive and scoop him up. I noticed cattle running all around me, close to me. I saw their shadows on the dark wet grass. I saw the hip of a red steer that was going to hit me before I could turn, and then I felt a jar and a shooting pain. From the ground I saw Barb ten feet away try to get up, get only his head up, and then fall back. A wave of cattle shut him out. A hoof struck my ankle bone as a hammer drives a nail and sent pain clear to the thigh. I smelled a horrible decaying odor of the ground itself, and then I saw Barb rise again, brace his forelegs, and stay sitting on his rump like a huge dog. He swiveled around upon himself to face the cattle and his ears went up sharp and clear against the sky, like two leaves. The steers gave way before him.

To me he wasn't a horse—he was an island glimpsed through the trough of the sea. Crab-fashion, on hands and knees, rolling and falling among the hoofs, I got to him, moving faster than ever in my life before; and as I came beside him, the next great living wave broke over us and went away on either side, as water does around a stone.

I shouted and brandished my hat. The cattle came on silently, loosely packed, so they could barely swerve and miss us. Barb's forelegs quivered. He kept putting a jerk in them to take that slack out, but, just when the flow of cattle had begun to thin, they snapped and let him down. Blood ran from his mouth where the bit had cut. I took the bridle off and watched Barb lie there, opening his mouth as the pain hit him, but I couldn't stand to see that and looked away.

Rollo Jane alone was keeping the cattle from King Tule, and how that boy did ride! I looked for Sims and saw him back on the tail of the herd, pretending to work hard, but he wasn't—he was afraid of that bad ground. The moon came out very bright, and far ahead I saw Dynamite fly over a piece of black marsh. Water from a pond he crossed shot up like silver sparks. He seemed to ride the air. And he was riding to win, he and Rollo, for with the help of Barb and me they'd bent the right flank south and pointed it for Oyster Neck. Two men there could bend her back along the Little Betty, and they were there. Rollo came down like six men upon those cattle. He was catching Dynamite, racing on the throat of the Neck and a little to one side, when all of a sudden he disappeared.

But Dynamite didn't know. He dashed onto the point of land and turned the leaders. I saw him leap a ditch and then another, quickly, and in the moonlight far away it looked as though his pony had begun to buck. He turned fifteen or twenty head and circled to do it again, and then he must have seen there was no use. Behind, where Rollo should have been, the cattle streamed away down Oyster Neck. Dynamite didn't quit. He charged back across those steers and back again, making shadowy lines of them shoot from the herd; but he was one alone and the job was too big. I could see his little nag fail, tripping once, and at last Dynamite pulled him up and stood there, making a long dark eddy in the flow of cattle.

Those steers never had run; they flowed like water pressed by some invisible hand, as the earth rises behind a mountain stream and sends the water down.

Still, if the fence held across the Neck, Dynamite would win. I remembered Jim Magee, the construction boss, telling of the stout fence he had built on Oyster Neck to keep the cattle from the bluff and the bogs along the water; and down where the point of land narrowed I could see a black mass of steers damming up and knew the wires had stopped them—or was it board? I couldn't remember. Behind that dam the dark area of steers grew and grew, swirling in the moonlight slowly and more slowly, until they almost stopped; and then there came a sound ringing like a shot and then another and then a volley of them, and I saw the cattle release slowly down the Neck. They gained in speed, frightened by the crash of splintering wood, pressed forward by the wind, running silently, with never a sound since the moment they began to move. The lead steers spread out singly on the bluff, clear against the sky, and behind them two thousand pairs of stubby horns were coming to find shelter from that wind; and in the bottom of the bay they found it.

I watched them go. I thought I heard waves breaking on a beach, and the sound grew and the wind took it away and brought it back louder than before, undulating, alive, and then I knew it was the moaning of the cattle as they broke in waves upon the rock and died. . . .

Sims rode up to me and said, "Have a spill?"

"Yeah," I said, "I've had a spill."

Barb was quiet now, poor devil, but every so often he gave a kind of shiver as the pain took him. I asked Sims if there was a gun in the bunkhouse, and he said one of the farm boys had a forty-five. I pointed out where Rollo had fallen and told him to get over there. He went, loping his mare like he'd ridden on marsh ground all his life.

I saw Dynamite riding back from the Neck. He didn't even look after those cattle, but went off with Sims into a shadow and I couldn't see what they were doing. After a long time Dynamite rode up to me and sat against the moon, with the wind tugging the brim of his hat; and when he saw Old Barb, I could hear him choke. He said they had found Rollo lying with a broken collarbone at the edge of a peat burn; his horse had been too heavy to get out and had smothered. Then he looked at Barb again, and all he could do was swear a little softly and say to me, "Well, dammit, we made our ride; that's all a feller can do."

He started for the bunkhouse to get a car and a bottle of whisky for Rollo, and I told him to find me a gun. Then Barb and I waited alone. The night wore away and a rim of light came up along the east, as though out there a thousand miles somebody had kindled a fire. Everything I heard became an echo, which is what happens when you're very tired, and that made the island a queer place—as though all over it hundreds of people were trying to talk in different languages. Barb got restless and wanted to stand up, so I sat on his head. I wished Dynamite would come. Barb had his mouth open and would put one eye on me as he took a deep swallow of air. He didn't look like my horse at all, down in the rotten mud that way with me sitting on his head. I didn't want to remember him like that.

The lights of a car turned up the Little Betty and pretty soon Dynamite came on foot. He carried an ivory-handled forty-five with a bright silver barrel, and said for me to hold the bottle of whisky while he used the gun.

"Give me the gun," I said.

"No," he said, "I'll do it."

"Give me the gun," I said.

"Why, you silly kid . . . you don't know how to shoot a horse. You likely never shot a horse in your life."

I held out my hand and he gave me the gun. As I walked around in front of Barb, moonlight reflected from the silver barrel. I thought: "What a silly gun. This is the kind of gun with which men perform tricks at a circus. I can't shoot my horse with it." Then I whistled and Old Barb raised his head. I drew the imaginary lines from each ear to the opposite eye and pulled the trigger at where they crossed.

"Good shot," said Dynamite.

After breakfast we sent Sims with Rollo to the doctor; I took his Appaloosa mare and rode with Dynamite for Oyster Neck to see what had happened. I wasn't feeling very happy. The wind had blown itself away and only a breeze, gentle as May, floated some delicate white clouds. We followed the auto ruts along the Little Betty that Jim Magee had made the summer before when he hauled lumber for the fence, and that ran far from the place I didn't want to see. We found the fence splintered to pieces. Dynamite thought there would be crippled cattle on the rocks, perhaps some that were unhurt, and we were starting for the bluff when a horn sounded behind and we saw a pick-up truck bouncing over the field. I thought it was Rube come to say "I told you so," but this time it was T. S. Ordway himself with Jacks, his foreman, at the wheel, and Jim Magee sitting on a box behind.

Jacks looked the same as ever—well-tanned leather doesn't change—but I had expected signs of concern on the face of T. S. Ordway. After all, sixty thousand dollars doesn't run right off the books every night. He sat looking straight ahead out the windshield. He wore the same city hat and tweed coat that looked grown onto him as all his clothes did, as though he never took them off. He was talking to Jacks about a bridge he planned to build across the slough. He waved to us without interrupting himself and sat there watching the distance, deliberately saying every word as men do who are used to having people listen. The new bridge, he said, would cost thirty-five thousand dollars, but by doing away with the barges and the ferry it would in the long run save money.

Jim Magee climbed off his seat and stood beside the truck. T.S. stopped talking and looked faraway at nothing, as he always did when he had a lot on his mind, and then he said to me, "Boy, I'm sorry you lost your horse."

That made me feel better because all at once I remembered Barb had been his horse, not mine.

Now he said to Jim Magee, "Guess we'll have to build a stouter fence—eh, Jim?"

Jim agreed to that but the Old Man said no more; he was talking to Jacks again about the bridge. "I'd like to see it made of concrete piers; they would last longer.

Let's go back now and see if that bottom will take concrete."

Jim climbed aboard and they drove away. Half a mile down the field the car stopped and we could see T.S. and Jim stand beside it and put their heads together, looking up now and then and pointing off across the field, and we knew T. S. Ordway had thought of something else to build.

Dynamite reached thoughtfully through his pockets to find the dirty plug of tobacco he always carried; and as he fished it out, he brought up with it the big idea for which he had been searching.

"One thing here you can be sure," he said; "you're working for a great man."

ALL IN A DAY

The El Dorado Investment Company lay still. Thomas Ordway, its builder, owner, and sole proprietor, was dead. Out of respect to him the men had been given a half-holiday.

So we sat around the door of the blacksmith shop feeling the good sun on our necks and watching Argo, the radical Slav, as he bored holes with a drill press in an iron bar. Easter day had come out fair, with a light wind blowing from the north that cleared away the delta mist and let the sloughs sparkle early, and the river, and the long tule reeds that carry up sunlight from the water when the north wind blows. A bright finger of this sun reached in to Argo where he stood, bent like a shaggy tree above the press to see just how the drill curled back the silver shavings from the bar, the drawbar that in six weeks or maybe seven would pull the binder to reap and tie the grain of Thomas Ordway, now dead.

We kidded Argo for working Easter Sunday.

He said, "You crazy, boy, looka the grain."

Well, that was pretty funny. Grain at Easter doesn't stand eight inches high. It sprouts up there against the yards as suburbs in the spring grow green around a city, and the wind flows on it slow like water. It's a sight to see, true, but it will be needing neither drawbar nor binder for a good long time. So when Argo waved another paw around his shop, and pointed out the sharpened mowing knives, the bundles of twine laid for the binder, Sims answered him and said, "Hell Argo, lay off. Rust'll take them knives; the mice'll have that twine ate up before the oats is in the milk. Sit down, have a smoke. Old Ordway's dead."

"Nosir, boy," said Argo. "Like I remember Mr. Ordway when I was working in the mill. . . ."

And Argo said that carefully to let us hear. Ever since Ordway had raised him from the mill and set him on the books at three-and-a-half a day instead of three dollars, Argo had spent time for pleasure in his blacksmith shop and had talked backward when he spoke about the mill, letting his voice fade a little and tire, as though the El Dorado's mill were a land far over the water—maybe Serbia, the place from which he had come.

". . . Warehouse number two; it is wintertime, the grain of summer is all gone, the hay is gone. It is nighttime and the trucks are coming—one, two, three—

all a night long to carry in hay Mr. Ordway has bought. When? When did he buy? Yesterday? Last week? Nosir, back in August, last July he estop in the field, at a warehouse; and if the price is five dollar, he make it four; and if six, he say five, because he talk by thousand dollars. Then he beat it away all over the country and you think he has forgotten. He do this thing, he do another, he go to Texas—and you think he has forgotten; but no, the hay must wait till *he* is ready. One day he takes a telephone, says, 'Gimme my hay!' Then a Diesels start a roll, and all day long and night the smoke goes up and down the roads; and in the little towns you hear 'em grind, you guys, and you say, 'Ordway's hay, El Dorado hay.' Who has paid money so the trucks can roll? Who has made his plan long-distance? Thomas Ordway! . . . First a truck gets in. Who is there? Thomas Ordway, three o'clock in the morning—no matter. 'Turn the lights, get a goddam mill crew. Hallo, hallo!' . . . So my job, it is the Stovers engine to hoist a bales up—little old thing spit-spit, one-and-a-half horses. So Mr. Ordway stand and watch and he stick a finger in the water-can to see how hot and he say, 'Argo, you lose a half-a-horse; I show you.' He stop everything; alla works. He gets Sammy and Jim Dill and we find leather laggings for those pulleys so they won't be slick where the belt goes round and round. 'Thatsa where you lose your horse,' he say, 'right in that slick. Hurry up, now Argo!' he say. 'You gotta catch that horse!' . . . Poochee, then the bales go up. Sure," said Argo. "When

Mr. Ordway walk through, there be something better afterwards, every time."

"Well he ain't walkin' no more," said Sims.

"Aw, he was big," said Rube. "When he fell, it was like a tree in the forest crashin'!"

Argo took his iron to the fire and cranked the handle till the sparks were dancing with the draft, and the old forge made a groaning and a sigh, and when he saw the coke was bright, he shoved the iron in.

"Reckon they've read the will?" said Cherokee.

"Even at that," said Jody, "I bet a feller *could* have learnt a lot from old T.S., watching him day by day."

"'Tain't days a feller leaves behind," said Sims, "it's ready cash. I learn that easy."

"Heard he was buried in his old deerskin jacket," said Rollo Jane. "That one he allus used to wear."

"Naw, hell," said Sims "he's gotta die receptacle; he done business in that jacket."

"That's what I heard Jacks tell," said Rollo, "after the funeral and he was right to him, could have touched him where he laid."

"Who do you reckon'll get the dough?" said Jody. "What'll happen to the El?"

"That's accordin'," said Sims. "Now some says he has it all divided in his will. Some says he never made no will, that the State gets it. And others says not so at all—the whole works goes for auction. So I dunno. I know for sure it's not for us."

"Wish't he left me a day off," said Jody. "That's all I'd ask. One Sunday regular."

"I 'spec I'll go to the Navy Yard," said Rollo Jane. "I can get a job there scaling anytime, knocking the rust off boilerplates—$5.28 a day to start."

"Wish't he'd left me what he's made a-working us Sundays," said Sims. "All I could carry would be enough."

"I'd just want a day," said Jody. "One regular I knowed was comin'. That's all I want."

"Yeah," said Sims, "and the people in Hell wants ice water, too." The wind blew us down from the cookhouse the sound of Mike, the cook, banging his triangle for lunch, and Jody stood up first and said, "Well, I've got a bottle; this is Sunday; I'd like to take a little drink before I eat, but I wouldn't care for it to be alone."

We took off for the bunkhouse—all but Argo; and Sims looked back and saw him at the anvil, throwing a kink in that drawbar; and Sims hollered back, "You better quit that, Argo! They're just now buryin' a guy who worked on Sunday."

DEATH IN OCTOBER

After the death of T. S. Ordway the El Dorado Investment Company continued as before. The mill ground just as much feed; the cattle in their pens went right on eating, getting fat, being sold at a good profit; and the boys that made the wheels go round were on the job at seven every morning when the whistle blew. They earned their three dollars; but at the end of the month the pay checks came out signed, not by T. S. Ordway, but by So-and-So, trustee.

One thing the great man never failed to do through all his wide realm of ownership was to sign the pay checks personally—hundreds of them. It cost him the last week of every month, but he did not complain. "I never paid a man in anything but cash," he said. "If I can't see his face, I want to know his name." You see, this was later in his career, when the meetings got in his way, the papers, dividends, and debentures.

After he died, the river ran on down. The days began out of the east, broke over the high Sierra, and passed on down with the river out to sea, just as they always had done. The great green delta on an afternoon swayed and muttered and lapped, as the wind played in the reeds around the islands—the islands with their levees built by Thomas Ordway, master-architect, who worked in earth, not wood or stone.

Yet after he went, there was a difference. People said so. Perhaps they looked for one; and where you seek, you find, as the Good Book says. But in the noises of the wind there was an echo as it talked across this wide city of boards and cattle; in the grinding of the mill there was an echo, a different sound when you listened. It seemed the feed-trucks moved more slowly, the men stopped more often to talk. Little things made a bigger difference. When steers went off a quarter of a cent, it was generally decided that the market would not have dared to do that in the time of T. S. Ordway. When school children passed through in caravans, and on Sundays when pleasure cars lined the county road that runs along the yards, the people made no sound, but looked with wide-open eyes, for this might be the last time anyone would see the El Dorado Investment Company, about which everybody had heard.

In the bunkhouse, in the cookhouse, we wondered

what was going to happen. During the day we gathered often at the barn to talk—the old gray shelter, eaten by the wind and rain, that was a derelict when T. S. Ordway found it standing on a mound above the sloughs. There he had his dream and built his city out of mud and reeds, the richest land in all the world, where wealth lay in the decay of centuries, alluvium, waiting for a man who could see, but waiting not alone, as we found out.

Day after day strange cars glided up and down the alleys, filled with men in city suits smoking good cigars—trustees, appraisers, inspectors, heirs nobody ever had seen—all of them foreigners that didn't belong. It hurt you some way just to see them. Rumors came with every car-load: the yards were being sold for taxes to Swift, to Armour, to the government for an experiment in cattle like those they had made in electricity. But nobody knew.

All that summer was unusually cool. Sea fogs blew in and lay all day. On clear evenings after sunset, off westward toward the blue hills, a cloud formation was observed several times like a great red spear thrust in the sky; and people said this was a sign, and others said it was because of the war raging far over the sea.

Archibald Jacks ran the yards as he had always done, but his shoulders drooped a little and there was no smile in him. Reuben Child, earliest made and latest left of all the helpers of the great man, came to the barn the first few days and lingered like an old dog around the place he had seen his master last; and then he left and was seen no more. At evening his white cottage by the slough had no light; and some said he had gone away into the hills to die, and some said he had gone back home to Texas where he had been born so long ago and where he had first met Thomas Ordway.

Summer blended into fall, the lonely time of year. The days came hot and still, with a hush and everlasting echo, and the sound of wind passing somewhere up above that never touched the earth. From the ventilator on the mill dust rose and spread a fan across the sky. You could hear the heavy, hollow grinding of the gears digesting cattle feed. . . . The things T.S. had set going kept on after him.

Daylight on those mornings found dry ground. There was no dew, no night that mattered. No wind blew, yet in the reeds there was a rattle dry as death. You could hear the endless roaring of a tractor in the fields beside the river where it dragged a great disk plough to break the ground for next year's crop, and here a shroud of yellow dust rose up and hung above the field.

On the sixth day of October the great disks ripped open an Indian burial mound and the skeletons came up like white roots out of the ground. For a day or two there was a good deal of excitement over this, because the sixth came on a Friday, and during the week end people from Bird Town and the nearest villages came down to collect trophies. Later all this was carefully remembered and retold, together with the facts that cats had eaten grass and for three nights straight a ring had lain around the moon. But for the moment the novelty passed and would have been forgotten except for what happened Monday.

Ten minutes after ten the anthrax struck. The first steer went down in Pen 78, close beside the water, and a little blood ran from its nose. Pen 77 was next, the steers dropping as if they had been poled over. Few lived more than half an hour. Not till afternoon did we know what they had. There had been no anthrax in the valley for fifty years. The veterinary stocked no serum; he wired San Francisco.

Old Jacks cruised around the alleys in his pick-up looking the way he did the afternoon news of Ordway's death was brought to him.

The cattle dropped like flies. All Monday night we stood and heard them moving in the dark, kicking in the dust a little when they fell, and soon all would be quiet but for the restless moving of the other cattle up and down the pens. By morning the water troughs were ringed with dead.

Then the serum came and we went to vaccinating. All day long the columns of cattle choked the alleys, moving to the pens around the branding chute, and the yellow dust rose as it does from armies marching. There was no sound. This was the quiet death, taking some even as they moved to safety. Only the grinding of the mill went on; and the plough, breaking the land, its sound falling on the out-turn, coming louder on the way back; and over it the dust rose yellow too.

We put the needle into better than a thousand head a day, but thirteen thousand cattle take a lot of vaccinating. The biggest, fattest ones came first—they cost the most. Around the chute there was a milling red-and-dusty mass, the press and clatter of the cattle on the boards, the sharp bellow of pain as the needle stuck them, and the white-and-silver flash of Dynamite's bare forearm with the syringe, for it was he who did the vaccinating.

"Die and prove it!" he would yell, driving home the needle in the soft necks; and the steers would buck and squeal.

Nazi Joe was there, working the drop-gate at the far end of the chute where the cattle went out when Dynamite finished them. Joe was a roly-poly little old German with a battered dun-colored felt hat, stained with sweat, which he always managed to keep jaunty on his head, cocked up a bit behind, so that he looked like a poor Bavarian mountaineer. Actually Joe came out of Prussia, I think. He wore his shirtsleeves short, cut off at the elbows like a little boy's; his face was red from years of weathering and his eyes were as blue as Dynamite's, only they didn't move—they stuck and stared. A Dutchman stiff and stubborn, with a streak of astrology in him, Joe had a mind that was a whiz on a column of figures, but on other things got just so far on the right track—and then off into either air or water.

Uncle Arky Billy was there, Cherokee and Sims, and Jacks himself, coming and going in the pick-up, his face growing longer with the lines of cattle.

Outside in the alleys the dead-wagons went about their business hauling the bodies, chained behind in tandem, to the fields where they were piled with straw and gasoline, and burnt. Their smoke rose and mingled with the dust the tractor made, until the sun turned red and the stench of roasting meat hung in the air all day.

So it got to be the thirteenth, our lucky day, and we waited by the chute after our noon meal for Jacks to come. He said it was our lucky day; we had eleven hundred head to go, but he didn't come and he didn't come; so we talked it over and went ahead without him, Dynamite in charge. Since Ordway died, Jacks had been like a man walking in a dream, and all the yards for him were like a great house he had known well, furnished in a way he'd seen a thousand times, every chair in place—but nobody home. You'd find him sometimes in the evening sitting in his pick-up alone by the mill or on the docks where the barges tie up and leave their sacks of grain, where the hustle and the bustle is all day, with no time to think and remember. Jacks liked to find those places after work; there was no telling where he was now, so we went ahead.

"Stack 'em up, you guys!" sang Dynamite. "Cattle, *cattle,* ten head to a chute!" And Cherokee and Sims and I shoved them in with terrible shouts, waving our gunny sacks, shaking our sticks.

Dynamite worked from a platform built three feet off the ground along the chute. Uncle Arky Billy helped him, filling the syringes. Nazi Joe worked his drop-gate at the far end. He said slowly after a while, "Jacks, he got zee anthrax." Joe came out of Germany in 1912; his English still had a buzz in it.

"Anthrax?" said Dynamite. "You're crazy. Men, *zey* don't take anthrax."

"Yes, zey do too," said Joe, yanking down the bar that raised the gate. "Dat's just where you mistaken. Zee anthrax is one of zee most terrible diseases known to man."

"What makes you think he's got it?" said Dynamite to Joe; and to a steer: "Die, you son-of-a-bitch! Die and prove you're hurt!"

Joe kept right on, you couldn't put him off once he got track of an idea, and he never hurried and never let his voice get up or down: "Zee stars say it is his time."

"Stars! . . . Stars my foot; stars don't talk, they shine. Goddammit, Joe, you're gonna break your back out there by the cookhouse some night. I've seen you, bent like a barrel hoop."

"Zee stars never tell a lie," said Joe. "If you study dem, you would be money ahead of zee game. Take Jacks, he don't know, you see . . . October is his month.

In zee first part he stand good chance for success; in zee middle part, especially zee thirteenth day or fourteenth, he should be careful, watch his step. Zee stars never say 'You must' only 'You should' . . . there is a good chance of things to happen dis way, happen dat way."

"Horse-water," said Dynamite.

"Man," said Joe, "Man he is a product of zee sun. If he be born when sun is overhead, zee upright position of zee cornstalk, he has more chance for success; he be like a tide coming in. But October is not very good month, sun is changing, he is tired. . . . You find a quarter-shadow around noon. . . ."

"I bet you Jacks ain't got the anthrax," said Dynamite. "What makes you think he has?"

Sims piped up, "I seen a black sedan parked by his house at noon."

"Doctor Hartley's car," said Joe. "Jacks went into his room before lunch, lock zee door, don't let nobody in. They telephone zee doctor."

"You've been listening to that Thelma Jenkins' talk," said Dynamite. "I seen her coming to the cookhouse after noon to get her eggs and butter for Old Lady Jacks. You'd better not listen to her; she'll have you b'lieving stars is stripes before she's through."

There was no talking while Sims and I and Cherokee crammed home another chute.

"Anthrax is zee most terrible death," said Joe. "One time on 2 Street, Sacramento, last April ven I vas dere,

I talked vid a fellow who has only one eye; half his face vas cut away—you know—big scar. 'Vat's de matter your eye?' I says. 'Oh,' he says, 'I hadda anthrax.' 'How does dat disease operate?' I says. 'Very simple,' he says. 'Anthrax of zee human being is de most terrible disease. Once de germ is in de blood dere is no hope—only chance,' he says. He says he owns a bunch of cattle, one of dem die; him and anudder fellow, dey chop it up, zee knife slip, cut him on de hand, and dat vas de way zee germ obtain entrance to zee body. Dey rush to a doctor; doctor he say: 'Can do nudding; first we must follow zee germ.' He put him on de table, under zee X-ray. Venever zee germ come near surface of zee blood zey try to catch him. If he come to zee heart—too bad. Zis time dey have good luck; he come out in zee eye and zey catch him with a knife."

"God Almighty," said Dynamite, "I hope they don't do that to old Jacks."

"Maybe so, maybe not," said Joe. "Maybe he die. Remember der is nudding accomplished but vat der is destruction first."

Joe kind of had us there, and we thought a bit about many things, and Sims said half-aloud: "Jacks cut his hand this morning . . . on that steer, remember? He was cutting the screw-worm out of its back."

Jacks *had* nicked his hand; we all remembered.

"Once zee germ has entrance to zee human body," said Joe, "a man is gone. Dat is why information of zee stars is useful."

"The stars don't know that much," said Dynamite. "There ain't nobody knows about death only God Almighty."

Joe didn't answer; when he wanted to call you a liar, he could do it with the back of that blunt head of his, he was that stubborn.

"Nosir, Joe, you're full of hop and star dust," Dynamite went on. "Death ain't in the sky. . . . Death—death's like a lariat-rope and you're on one end and God, he's on t'other. You're born thataway, strung up; and that way you run your life. . . . Like I've let many a steer go along after I had him roped, till I found a place to bust him out; and then I took my dallies and made my pony squat and hold. Same with death—you have your run and take your spill. Ain't it so, Uncle Billy?"

"That's right, Dyney boy," the old Arkansawyer said. "Yessir, that's about it, I reckon, for the most part. We're on one end, God Almighty, Lord of Jacob, he's on the other. . . . Reckon he had time to repent?" said Uncle Billy. "Jacks, I mean. He weren't much of a church-going man, you know."

"Oh, I think he would," said Dynamite. "Jacks' heart was in the right place, though he could be ornery, the old son-of-a-gun. Many's the time I've wanted to warp his head with a neck-yoke. But I reckon if he has took off, he's up there now a-lookin' down on us boys."

"Sure hope so," said Uncle Billy. "*Sure* do."

Cherokee said, "You boys is sounding mighty high-falutin' in this here argyment, like you'd all been to college. Seems to me this death come right out of the ground."

Cherokee didn't often say much, but he made sense when he opened his mouth. We took a look around our feet, and I remember it was quiet just then, between two fillings of the chute, and you could see the tower of dust built by the plough and hear the tractor going faintly; and then, in a second, we got fear. Nobody said so; we just had it. It ran quicker than any disease; and we were looking at our hands for cuts and shifting on our feet without intending to, as though we stood on something hot.

Up Long Alley by the mill the boys were bringing us more cattle, the last ones, and their dust in the air looked worse than poison gas.

"Well, I dunno," said Dynamite, but his heart wasn't in it. "Cattle," he hollers. "Whatsa matter with you guys? Gimme some cattle." He grabbed a syringe from Uncle Billy and rolled his right sleeve up a notch as though he was ready for the anthrax then and there, by God.

We began to move slow motion.

Two trucks came up empty from the mill, whining on the turn of the road and passing us right by as they did a hundred times a day, but this was different—it seemed as though they were running from something.

"Here's your wife, Dynamite," said Sims.

The top-heavy Packard sedan rolled down the slope from the barn and made the dust burn with its brakes.

Maxine got out. She was in a hurry; there was a handkerchief across her face.

She ran and jumped up on the fence and leaned our way and she was screaming mad. "Don't any of you men come home!" she yelled. "Not one, not any one of you. . . . Sims, Annabelle told me to tell you; and Cherokee, your Mary says the same—it' *anthrax!* . . . Jacks has it! . . . He locked the door, wouldn't let them in, but they took the axe—No!" she said, seeing Dynamite start toward her. "*No,*" and it made your spine go cold to hear it, wife to man. "*Stay back!*"

Dynamite went all the faster.

Maxine was off that fence and into that car quicker than the light of day. She put her head outside and called back once, "You can't come near the babies; don't you *dare!*"

Dynamite stopped at the gate, looking after her and cussing.

Sims started to run.

"Where-ya-going?" Dynamite's voice would have taken off your ear.

"*The dust!*" screamed Sims.

Dynamite knocked him down and he rolled in the dust.

Cherokee said, "Say, Dyney—reckon we outta stop that plough, and them trailing cattle down the alley there? Don't you reckon we outta stop them just a while till we get all this straight?"

"We ain't a-stoppin' nothin'," said Dynamite.

Sims got up and looked like he wanted to run again,

but Dynamite said to him, "There'll be no running while I'm here, understand?"

"Listen," said Uncle Arky Billy, "listen, boys!"

We looked into the sky. There was no wind; the sun up there was red and evil as the heart of a boil. We listened, but the sound we tried to hear had gone. "The mill," said Cherokee. "She's quit."

"We ain't a quittin'," said Dynamite.

"It was the plough made the dust," said Sims, half-whimpery.

Now that the noise was gone, it seemed the air had died like a body does when the blood goes out of it. All those alleyways and mangers, all that valley, river, and the hills beyond were empty veins of air, and only the cattle moved or made a sound. Two were dead just beyond us in the holding pen, Bar-Seven steers.

Hank and Jerry, who'd been helping out there, had taken off. I saw them hurry out the back way behind the scales, up toward the barn. Uncle Billy filled a syringe, matter of fact as biscuits and ham-gravy. Nazi Joe tightened up a little in the face, but he stuck to the handle of his drop-gate, ready for that destruction he'd talked about.

"Lookie," said Dynamite, and his voice picked us up.

Gliding low, cruising down the alley from the barn, a pick-up truck was coming in just the easy way Jacks always drove.

The little truck stopped by the outer gate; the door opened and a man got out, but it wasn't Jacks or even his ghost. It was Reuben Child, whose day was gone, whose face was like the side of a mountain where the rains have been. "Howdy, fellers," he said. "Vaccinatin'?"

He hobbled over; he needed a cane to walk. "Understan' ye got the anthrax in your herd," he said, and hardly got his voice above a little girl's.

All his strength was in his face and eye, but he made you want to knock down mountains, that old Rube. "Just thought I'd lend a hand," he said. "Not doin' much these days."

We began to vaccinate.

"Haven't seen you lately, Rube," said Dynamite. "Where you been?"

"Me?" said Rube. "Oh, here-and-there."

He was looking mighty fit for a man who's just been here and there. Those wide gray eyes, always finding some horizon, had got hold of one they liked, and it had lit him up inside in a way we'd never seen. If Rube had been a drinking man, I'd have said he'd taken a few.

He held the syringes; Uncle Arky Billy, who, though he had good legs under him like old Rube, would never see sixty again, got out behind with us into the crowding pen, and then even Sims was ashamed and went to work. We crammed those cattle through. The dust rose up so thick you really couldn't see. Your face turned black; your hollers turned to croaks. We used up all the water in the bottles and didn't dare take the time to send for more.

The anthrax never slackened. It stole the cattle out from underneath our sticks. Here a heifer, there a steer—down like a hog with an axe on its head; then a twitch, a little blood. We let them lie, forgot about the dead-wagon not coming. The boys brought the last pens of cattle up Long Alley and took off without a word, drifting in the dust like shadows, but we never cared.

All of a sudden it got very dark. The wind that for two weeks had wandered up there trying to get down came now, and the dust was made up into sheets and spirals and went everywhere. The wind stopped; the dust cleared off and there was the sky all brown and rotten as though the wind had gone up there with all its dust. The first rain brought thunder. Then the sky broke open.

We wallowed in it, thankful at first, till we saw the mud sticking and thought of germs that live for fifty years, and then I think some of us would have prayed if we could, or had had the time. But things were happening. The cattle couldn't make the chute. The slick board bottom, polished by their hooves, greased with the mud and dung, was no good footing. They went down; they stacked up on one another. A little heifer broke her neck. We spent twenty minutes clearing out the chute, while thunder smashed the hills across the river and the raindrops hit us big as dimes.

Rube called it off. "There's one place we can go," he said, waving a cane toward the barn.

"Not with all these cattle," said Dynamite. "What good will it do? This here's the only chute."

"We'll use our loops," said Rube, "if we ain't forgot quite how. Otherwise these little cattle won't make it till morning. We only got two hundred left."

So we turned the others in the holding pens and took our two hundred little Double Arrow steers and drove them to the barn. We made the horse-corral a holding pen. We cleared the inside of the barn all across one end, moved the bales of hay, dragged an old harvester, kicked out some mangers so there was room to move between the walls from one side to the other, across thirty yards of dirt. This was our crowding pen.

We lit the lanterns and brought the little steers inside, a bunch at a time.

Rube said to Dynamite, "Get me your horse."

"Hell, Rube," said Dynamite, "better let me do the roping."

"I'll do her," the old man said.

We helped him onto Dynamite's renegade nag that might have got a pint of Texas Steeldust in him generations back. He hurt Rube; that broken hip hadn't been in a saddle for ten years, but the old man straightened himself up bit by bit. He wanted to do it. There was something about Rube this night we all remembered—a rising in him and a kind of light, and he moved clean-cut out of the air, smoothly, like he knew just where he was going.

Dynamite whispered, "Rube's sure ridin' high. What's

the matter with him? What's he got?" But at that time I didn't know myself.

He took his stand, old Rube, half-way along the mangers from the little steers, where they'd have to run between him and the wall, and began to build his loop; did it from the wrist, with a flick over and a flick back, and gave the signal down the barn for the boys to let the cattle come.

The wind blew the lantern light all cockeyed, splashed it on us, and rocked the barn and made the floor smoke dust.

Rube sat his horse. From Canada to Mexico his name was known; hardly a brand that hadn't felt his loop in olden days, Hooleyann or straight, and no maverick that ever ran was quicker than his hand and eye.

Dynamite and I stood back; Cherokee cut and pushed a little steer and let him scamper down the wall, under the lanterns, harness, and old blankets.

The hempen loop ran out like light, spun underhand, and ringed the yearling with a gentle slap. Rube had his dallies fast before the animal took a step. Dynamite put a loop on both hind-legs. I shot the syringe in the soft neck, handed the gun to Arky Billy, loosened Rube's rope, and pulled it off.

"That weren't so good," said Rube. "I meant to lay a figure-eight."

Next time he did, and the animal stepped through with right fore-foot and tied himself. Rube set him down without so much as a finger's help. And so on with the next and the next. Once we took a rest; once Rube missed a loop. Other than that, every throw but half-a-dozen was a perfect figure-eight; and Dynamite, on the ground waiting, had only to shake his head and smile, or lay down his rope to help me.

The two hundred-odd head took us so far into the night that we never knew how long it was.

The storm kept us company; and the tromping of the cattle, the rustle of the running loop, and the squeak and rubbing of Rube's saddle when his pony took a squat and laid the critters down.

The old man never showed his pain. The hours wore away and made him young. He took off the blue denim jumper and tightened his silver-studded belt, a prize from some rodeo long forgotten, and with the work he straightened in the saddle till the patient smile we always knew him by had gone and he wasn't bearing something any more—he was doing it himself.

I wish I could tell just how he looked. Nobody could who hasn't seen a man inside his job or a woman with a child.

We finished and the little steers that had begun at one end of the barn were all crowded at the other.

"Turn 'em out," said Rube. "Let the rain have 'em; the anthrax never will."

We sat along the bench by the door where the boss's saddle hangs, along with some pairs of extra stirrups, a couple of bits, and a strip of hose for ramming down the throats of critters when they choke.

"Death?" said Dynamite to Rube, one eye on Nazi Joe. "You sure beat him out of that one, Rube. Your loop is quicker than the Evil Eye."

Rube was tired; he smiled now the old way.

"Hurt your hip any?" said Cherokee.

"Little," said Rube, "but shucks, just shows what a feller can do when he wants. I should have been on a horse years back."

"How come," said Dynamite, "how come ye took to it tonight?"

"Oh, I dunno," said Rube, lifting his Stetson and wiping his high white forehead where the sun never reached. "I dunno . . . I guess because I had a dream."

"A dream?" said Dynamite.

"Yeah," said Rube. "Funny, my old daddy had one like it years ago, spring of '92, I think it was, or '93. We trailed 'em from the Pecos to Wyoming, two thousand longhorn steers and Dad and me and eight good boys. Crossed the Republican River on the first of May. That night we bedded on a grassy knoll by water where the bluestem went for miles knee-high to horse and man. We bedded just at dark after a long day and laid the wagon tongue for the North Star so we could find the morning's trail.

"I remember how old Tigue, the cook, got out his Dutch oven that night, wiped it with his special cloth made of a flour sack, and baked us bread—bread and beans and jerky stew. We lived like kings.

"Dad dreamed that night. Some way he was in a

house alone, a room all bare but warm. It was late afternoon, 'bout four o'clock. From where he sat there was a window and a quarter-angle view up a long rise to some blue hills where night was beginning to gather and creep down. That ground was funny too; it was all bare, low brush and stones.

"He set quite a while, he said, wondering why nobody come and then he realized that house was empty, bare and empty as a house can be, yet full of yellow light . . . the afternoon, you know. And as he set and got his view out quartering from the window in a long slice up, it seemed he just couldn't quite see enough, that just around the edges of that window was the home he knew; the green alfalfa patch, the orchard trees, the good red barn and horses standing, the windmill pumping water—ker-blong ker-chug, ker-chug ker-blong—and the spatter from the leaky leathers as it hit the stones.

"There was all this goodness just on either side of where he looked, but that slice of ground he had to see, it was just a desert, bare as anything, with night creeping down along it 'mongst the little stones.

"Seemed like the sun'd set already, he says, but he couldn't figure it, felt sure it was just four o'clock, half-day half-night.

"So he set. He waited a long time, said he never did know why, wanted to get up and look around the edges of that window and see all the good things he heard and smelt and knew was there, but he just couldn't do it. Said he began to listen for something, something special, and then he heard it coming on the walk outside, crunching in the gravel step by step, heard the door open and latch shut and the jingle of spurs hung on the buckhorn by the wall.

"And then he said he *knew* and he felt happy. D'rectly the steps come near and give him leave to look and there stood his old daddy, and his face was all one smile like he was powerful glad to see his son again. He touched my daddy's shoulder and just says, 'Howdy, Son!' . . .

"This was the dream my daddy had that night," said Rube. "At daylight we moved on. In seven days he died, and far in old Wyoming, on the Crazy Woman beyond Ten Sleep, we laid him in the ground."

Rube stopped talking, but outside the wind kept on, lightly now, with a good deal of rain in it. The gusts caught water falling from the gutter that runs along the eaves, and hammered it against the barn one second and let it slosh on down the next. Rube began rolling a cigarette. He never used two hands. We watched him roll and lick and smear the tangled weed-and-paper, then hold a match until it glowed.

"That was the dream you had?" said Dynamite.

"That was the dream I had," said Rube. . . . And after a while: "Well, reckon I'll call on Jacks before I go along. He's poorly; took the chickenpox, you know."

The HAPPY MAN

In the tradition of Frank Norris and John Steinbeck, Robert Easton's acclaimed first novel, published in 1943 only four years after *The Grapes of Wrath*, places Steinbeck's migrant farm and ranch workers in new perspective against a uniquely California scene. Easton and Steinbeck shared the same editor, the distinguished Pascal Covici of Viking Press. Frequently anthologized, now in effect part of Easton's ongoing Saga of California® series of historical novels, including *This Promised Land* and *Power and Glory*, this classic of Western American literature is reissued in new format with an introduction by Jack Schaefer, author of *Shane*, and a foreword by author-scholar-critic Gerald Haslam.